I0629838

Land and Soul

Wagner Olivo

Land and Soul

Land and Soul
Copyright © 2013 by Wagner Olivo

ISBN—13:   978—0615808697
ISBN—10:   0615808697

Registered in USA

Dedication

I dedicate this book to God and those who are part of his glory.

Land and Soul

A glossary has been provided in the back of the book. You could also visit the website **www.landandsoul.net** for interactions with other readers. Enjoy it!

Land and Soul

Dream and Genesis

I

O Muse, recount to me the dreams I vividly felt in
these two restless nights; or tell me in your own
way why did that beautiful and noble princess,
accompanied by such a distinguished gentleman,
appear to me in those dreams of mine?

In that first dream the princess's mirage disappeared
into the non-existing world and the gentleman's
apparition was also going away, but I, I did not
permit him to disappear; I kept him briefly, only
with the vigor of your desired existence.

=======================================

Now my lord, dressed in cassock, approaches me,
and I see him more clearly. The darkness disappears
and I see the immense church in front of me; it
looks exaggeratedly painted, as if it were the
imitation of a theatrical scenario with distorted
colors.

"O, father, kind and true humanist, tell me, who was that woman whom has left my soul restless and whose blood, although fictional, pushes me from side to side, and why did her eyes see in me the holy mercy?" I ask him.

He tells me: "My son, I left briefly notes, for you and for all men and women of your time and of mine, unfolding the atrocities that her noble people suffered, and it hurts me to hear from your own words that the tutors of my birthplace, influenced by a non-guilty conscience, or simply ignorance, would like to deny or erase the evil conquest and actions that led to the absolute elimination of the race of that benevolent princess of yours. Now, my briefly related account is considered an exaggeration by the modern people of my land and of your land; even though there's no community or individual pure Taino in the conquered land; and we know that the reasons were illnesses, hunger, sadness, fire, and the **sword**. She saw in you stratum of mercy because she believes that her almighty God hid in your own veins her dear blood; the blood that she is still shedding in the vision of those who reject injustice in the world; she also saw that a good thing never dies; that is, her Taino soul."

Again the good man's image fades and I exclaim for him to stay with me, but his voice becomes weak in the air while I try to listen to his words: "Summon the great Taino poetess, the princess in your dream, and tell her to recount for you the story that you seek."

=======================================

The darkness and the fog spread quickly on the earth and that father's mirage disappears. The wall of the church begins to evaporate swiftly as when a white sheet of printing paper catches a fierce fire and all its material vanishes into thin air. I keep standing in the same place, but now, now I am among trees so green that my soul feels relieved and everything feels happy. The sound of smooth and light steps attracts me and I turn my face passively towards it; I see at a short distance the mere poetess Anacaona.

The splendor of the Taino princess illuminates the contours of her suave, majestic cinnamon color complexion. Two large Taino braids descend from her head and rest on her breasts. Her breasts are covered with the skin of an Amazon beast, unknown and never seen by her own shining brown eyes; this piece of garment was cured with ancient fire. Her Taino skirt, made of crocodile shredded skin from her sacred land, cured in the same way as her breast layer, descends and lands just above her knees—an abomination for an old-world man; extreme flirtation for an old-world woman; a simple and adequate fashion for a Taino woman; and a godly bless for a Taino man.

I see two proud and strong Taino chiefs accompanying the princess. They look brave, but friendly and harmless.

4

"Come, do not be afraid, come and join us," says the warrior on her right. The other chief beckons me and with a smile invites me to join them as well; the princess smiles, too. I feel myself among friends. They turn around and head towards the forest; meanwhile a light and amicable titter pushes me towards them; it tickles me and I feel a predestination to follow them.

I am led to a cascade hidden deep in the woods. A freshwater pond forms right where the water lands; and Taino small children jump from a tree that curves towards the deepest part of the creek; they shout playfully and freely and unafraid.

I see dispersed adults carrying firewood for the nightly fire and warriors smeared with black color on their cheeks; it will combat the fervor of their most furious friend, the one that shines perpetually in the blue pinnacle of nature. Not far from us, there are hidden small Taino shacks. There's a big one to the north of us; it is different from the others; it has white new fronds covering the top; the straws were recompiled voluntarily and given to the princess by young subjects, given as a grace for the communal genius of their beautiful princess.

There's another hut directly to the south of us, twin of the first big one, hiding in its belly the yet immortal *Guamalú*, who has been battered by the years, on the brink of oblivion, but still strongly tied, for many generations, to the first children of

the immortal, relentless, intrepid, beautiful
Quisqueya.

The three hosts, kind with the utmost warmth,
sit on a white rock, where the dew from the
cascade refreshes their souls. The three of them
together extend their arms and expect me to sit
in front of them without fear, and they also expect
me to honor their courtesy.

"Come, my son, and tell me how to satisfy your
curiosity," she says.

I am encouraged by her tone of voice and say: "Tell
me your story, go as far and as remotely as you can,
and tell me your origin as purely as it is stored in
your brain. Tell me of your time of joy and your
time of sadness, and culminate with the births, lives,
and deaths of the great chiefs from all the Caribbean
Sea."

She begins: "O, my son, we are older than your
own, as humane as the best, as curious as your
instincts. We are children of the sun and the earth;
lovers of the fresh water of the lake; we're careful
of the furious sea; and we live with the benevolent
and destructive gods of men and goddess of nature.

"Our first ancestors lived in the mountain, in a cave
now hidden by the god of time, now sacred only in
our thoughts, but yet alive, strong, and
indestructible. The hollow is the cradle of the Taino

people. There, the god of blood and body to the Kiskeyans gave their souls.

"*Cauta* is illusory, but it is said that *Atabey*, the queen of the universe, fermented the air, the water, and the dust, and Yucahu, master of the sky and of thoughts, the only child of time, the son of the mother that nobody can see, burst his breath and gave invisible fire to the first people of Cacibajagua, the cave of the living souls.

"There the first Taino tribe grew, men and women, afraid of the sun and the distance. Macocael was the first to come out of the cave and he discovered the world in which we were to live. His fear was so great that he thought he saw Yucahu's image in the air. Frightened by the unknown vastness of the world, he returned trembling to Cacibajagua. Immediately, the first chief decreed that no one was allowed to leave the holy cave, and since that day, the main entrance to the cavern was under his command.

"Pious Macocael rose in the morning to reap the fruits of the trees of the fertile mountain. He would return to the cave with bundles of fruits, vegetables, and small birds and distribute the food to the graceful tribe; he supported a clan that was exaggeratedly growing in size and in ideology.

"The Tainos, grateful, but anxious in mind, knelt to venerate Macocael's caring actions. But a daring woman stayed standing and begged her chief for

7

compassion and liberation: she wanted him to allow
the tribe to wander freely in the mountain and to
appreciate the sunlight for he has created stories that
taught them that it was their right to enjoy nature's
wonders. So, Macocael's silence was broken.

"The tribe was silence and the chief said: 'Look up
to Yucahu, master of the sun and the sky, and
perhaps he will concede to your desire. He is the
only one who can get you out of here to a better
habitat. He is your true thoughts and your best
desire. As of for me, I think I just follow Yucahu's
order; I am only protecting his sacred people.
Tomorrow, I will pray and ask him to help you, and
Yucahu will decide your future. Do not be surprised
at mine.'

"The whole night, while guarding the entrance, he
asked Yucahu to enlighten him. He drew his face on
a stone and went away to try to find a place to
distribute the tribe. He descended from the
mountain and never returned. The Tainos, scared,
came out and saw the face of the pious and kind
spirit on the stone and closed the huge door and
fearing said: 'Macocael disobeyed Yucahu, and
look, there in the entry he was converted into a
stone, for this is all we know about him. Pray to
Yucahu so that he can protect us from the spirits
that live in Amayauna, the damned and dreadful
cave in Macocael's stories.'

"Guacanael took over as chief and went out to the
wilderness to work as tribal protector and provider.

But before he left, he said to the tribe: 'Do not be afraid of new things; some are good and some are incomprehensible. Let Yucahu be with you as he is always with me. If I am not back by midnight, it is because I am happier somewhere else and it is the wish of my god, Yucahu. Perhaps you should follow my steps; my face should remind you of my saying if it be the truth.' So, he spent some time admiring the distance, the space and the sun. He gladly gathered the fruits and the vegetables and brought them to the entrance of the cave, and even though he had completed his task earlier than expected, he waited outside thinking of the beautiful world that he had discovered. When night came, he wasn't satisfied with the present situation of the people in the cave. He knelt in front of a tree and piously implored the god of the land; he begged permission to take the tribe out of the cave so that they could explore the beauties in the island. Later he entered the cave and distributed the food and told his people: 'The solution to the shortest of space in the holy cave is outside in the wilderness. It is safe. Macocael wasn't right, it is your responsibility to look after your sons and daughters; a man by himself cannot sustain the needs of this tribe for long. Explore the world of Yucahu, and he will provide you with whatever you need.'

"Murmurs spread throughout the cave. Macocael had the best intention for the tribe; he had provided food and ideas and kept the tribe alive. Guacanael, the strongest and wisest of the people in the cave, did not want to fulfill his responsibility of provider and protector of the people. Those were the infamous rumors.

"The next day, Guacanael went out and delightfully worked under the lovely sun. Before nightfall, he again knelt in front of the same tree and many images came to his mind; he fell asleep in front of the cave. That night he did not enter the cavern and none of the Tainos came out. In the morning Yucahu entered his mind, and he was moved by the god's presence. He stood up and Yucahu showed him the horizon where he could see the entrance of the fervent sun. He drew his face in the bush closest to the cave, and his curiosity pushed him into the woods, where he discovered more beautiful things and for his vision, amazing. He never returned and the naked pious Tainos came out of the holy cave.

"'Behold!' a pious man said. 'Guacanael disobeyed Yucahu, and now he is converted into a tree. How can we understand the meaning of the images?' They came back into the cave, and it is said that the same disobedience brought damnations or blessings to several people who were turned into fruits, reptiles, insects and birds; some were captured by foreign spirits and some by their own indifference.

"Fear cornered the pious Tainos the day that Guacanael disappeared. Yet, they united to get strength and they danced the first naturally choreographically dance in Kiskeya, praising the god of miracles. Days passed and Yucahu disguised himself as hunger and entered the cave. He

tormented the innocent vulnerable Taino children.
Equally, he embedded courage in a woman, mother
and lover of some of the suffering youngsters.
Challenging Fear itself, the woman stood up in front
of her people and said: 'Yucahu, incorporeal king of
the Taino, came into our cave and has made this
hollow sacred and worthy of praise. We must come
out of the cave together and Yucahu will walk
together with us, and be with us until the end of our
days. He will show us unknown beauties as
Guacanael had suggested, and he will give us fruits
and veggies, those that will fill our bellies, and we
will honorably name our main source of food,
Yucca, and the place where we will gather to pray
and celebrate life, we will name *batey*, to honor
Yucahu's mother; because she is the goddess of
unity, fraternity, the creator of our universe, a
unique sacred being, invisible, lover of the good
people and the most compassionate; she is the main
element of the images that feed our spirits.'

"The sharp cry of hunger became high hope. They
took white stones, pieces of wood, and bits of gold,
which abounded in the cave; and these objects
became the first sacred statuettes, representing the
zemies who would rule their inner world. So, they
held each other hands and left the holy place
together with their gods. The fresh air detached fear
from their souls, and joy parted their hands while
the blessed Cauta provided them with its healthy
fruits.

11

"Leisure in the mountain made time fly, and a gigantic shadow clothed the earth; the Tainos descended and conglomerated in the beautiful valley. They collected pieces of wood, leaves, and some stones. Then they set fire to the sticks and the dry leaves and choreographically danced to the sound of the light voices of the Taino women, followed by the men's graceful pious voices: 'Yucahu, Yucahu, Yucahu—Yucahu, Yucahu, Yucahu, holy spirit, holy spirit, holy spirit.'

"They were submerged in the spirit of the union and the fire. When they finished their dancing round, each sat in the circle of fire, one after the other, as if they had rehearsed the dance for hundreds of years, and it all ended in silence.

"A heavy sleep invaded the fire site and defeated the tired eyes of the small children who did not want to part from their mothers and wanted to stay awake. One by one blinked with heavy sleep on their eyelids and one by one rolled their body, each hugging their respective mother, and soon the gentle sleep possessed them completely.

"A passive breeze disturbed the night and mysteriously shook the leaves of the Cibao's trees; *Guatauba* was hiding among those leaves; the messenger of the god agitated the minds of five of the bravest and smartest men in the tribe. The five of them were very spirited and independent. They broke the silence and each praised the compassionate and generous god and the illustrious goddess of theirs.

"Cibael was the first one to stand up and to speak to the crowd. His lineage extended onwards to that of Guarionex—affectionate, friendly, and beloved chief from La Vega—beautiful and fertile land; optimal peaceful haven, hidden by the shadow of Cacibajagua—land of fresh rivers, where gold shines among the pebbles of the suave streams.

"Guatauba propelled the words that came out of Cibael's mouth. 'Brethren, god loving people, let us first give thanks to the holy God, Yucahu, who is in all places—a being without beginning or end—the only being that no one has seen or will see, because its substance is ethereal and our eyes are captivators of earthly things. For that reason, I believe that the highest nobility, worthy of praise, will send us the zemies—angels and demons of the true god, and through them we will minimally grasp spiritual visions. Yucahu is in all minds, dressed up in all the images. Yucahu will make us stronger as a people, but only if we live and experience him in different places. For my part, I will take those who want to follow me to the north. They—my brothers, sisters, and children—will be free to choose their zemies as Maorocoti, the wisest being, will present them in life. Let us thank our god once again. Thanks, Divine Spirit who lives in heaven! You were conceived purposely by your divine mother—the creator of all material things, such as the moon, the

13

sun, and the sea. Protect us all the time that we spend on the earth!'

"Thus spoke Cibael in front of the beloved Taino congregation. Tears were shed and some souls felt and looked afflicted by the separatist mention. Cibael lowered his head to signify that he, too, was afflicted; he understood their worry, but then, he lifted his face to the heavens and held in his hand the first white stone that came out of Cacibajagua; and it was understood by this spirited symbol that the *Mother Stone* would be his goddess. He then cleansed the stone with crystal water and it was also understood that he would call his land *Magua*; and the name of his goddess, *Guacar*, was shouted from within the circle of fire.

"Cibael took his place in the circle of fire and invited the humble Marieanel to the floor. The first in the lineage of the chief Guacanarix stood up stronger, more pious, and more loyal to his people than any of his upcoming posterities. 'Oh, goddess, mother of Yucahu, your essence feels nubile every morning of my awakening and at night I see you in the astral beings, and still I appreciate you so little. I experience your marriage with the new day, and you provide us with fresh air coming from your bowels, and for being so simple in thoughts, I now feel that I don't thank you enough. You, goddess of the universe, Mother Stone of Cibael, essence of the earth, again, allow me to thank you and to name you Mother *Iermao* of Marien. I will take your statuette of goddess where you will also be known as the kindest of the North.

"'O, Yucahu, allow me to conserve this *Body of Stone*, for she is the mother that creates everything perfectly with her patience; a mother without beginning and more durable than the statue in my hand. You, Yucahu, master of the sun and fertilizer of the land, also instigator of the human actions under your sky, consent my words to thank you always at dawn when *Bajacu* emerges blithely in the morning over the horizon and starts warming your water, your plants, and all your beings. Please listen to my prayers and my thanks when Bajacu mysteriously disappears at nightfall, too.

"'Tainos, brothers and sisters, remember that in the North you will always have a friend, a father, a soul that will always pray for our well-being and our union; I will always love you and receive you with affection in Guárico—the forethought town of my goddess. Let me give thanks again to my god Yucahu and the kind Mother Iermao for their generosity,' so ended Marieanel. He also lifted his goddess to the heaven and took his place in the circle of fire.

"Nacanarocoel, alias Naca, took a step toward the light source. He said: 'My people, great is the God that has allowed us to spend this beautiful night together. If we have always given our holy god a common name, Yucahu, why do we now give our common Mother different names? She is supposed to be unity, fraternity, and kindness; creator of the universe; the earth; the water; and the creator of all material things. Why do we have to differentiate her now? Think well the derivation of this prophetic holy night. I have been given no choice but to name my goddess, your goddess, Apito, because she will be the goddess of my land, which will be named Maguana. The *First Mother of Stone* will be honored by my brave people. But, please, brothers and sisters, do not forget that our goddess belongs to all of us and she is only one.'

"He lowered his head and looked very disappointed. He didn't lift his goddess to the heaven; instead he hugged her on his chest and ceded his place to Cacarocayoa—Mother of Cayacoa's lineage. She stood in front of the campfire and said: 'Mother, goddess of the universe, I venerate you a lot, and I will call you by name Atabeira; because if the holy stone is durable, you are even more durable, and even more, you are the *Mother of the Original Stone*. I will protect you and will carry you to my land, Higüey. I will make Higüey a land of peace and a land of sentimentality. Tainos, there in my land, there will always be prayers for you. Visit us and we will always receive you with a fraternal embrace, love, and affection. Let our goddess live forever and she will always protect us from evil.'

"Thus spoke Cacarocayoa. She yielded to Yaguanael, alias the Great Yagua, the most verbal, the most prophetic, the bravest, master of Jaragua—

the most notable and outstanding of the chiefdoms—progenitor of the Bohechio's lineage and his descendants.

"He said: 'Yucahu, father of heaven and of earth, being without beginning and without end; no one can pinpoint your divine beginning, and I wonder, who can predict your end? Thanks for making me as I am, of flesh and bones, of blood and thoughts. I understand that in my temple you implanted a transient spirit, which believes himself to be an eternal owner of the blood that goes through the hot veins of my body; it feels unhurt when inadvertently the body loses a hand or leg or any of its part— uncorrupted until it reaches its half-life with time, and it begins to show its age in the way it thinks; yet it feels young in old age. You, Yucahu, you have shown me how matter and essence coexist, and you know why your mother has given each its due time; the soul grows old and it returns to a state of childhood until it fades and disappears as the essence of fire does. So, I say to you, my people, enjoy the goodness of Yucahu for surely time is slipping away from us. Tonight, we talk about a goddess who is many—Apito, Atabeira, Aguacar, together with the famous Iermao are venerated—and she is only our common Atabey. I am also glad to have my own goddess, the powerful Zuimaco, who will come from the union of two sects—created in the belly of Cacibajagua. One of my spouses will come from one sect and my soul is already dedicated to the other sect; but with time Zuimaco

17

will glue them unnoticeably into one; so it has already been agreed.

"'Yucahu is very much with me. Before tonight, I have met people who were different from me, and we all lived together in Cacibajagua. Some of you think that that difference makes us weak, and mistakenly you have already begun to tread on a gloomy grassy path. Jaragua will welcome everyone; differences and diversities will make us strong.

"'My people, today we talk about religious wars. We offer ourselves friendship, but this holy day— Yucahu has disguised it genially, for decades have swiftly gone beyond the time we left Cacibajagua— I have seen how the proud little girls proclaim in their games to have the best, the most clever and unique goddess. The little boys talk about the time when their god will come to this earth—dressed differently, mounted on a beautiful being from another land, coming with many angels and weapons from the sky. Oh, Tainos, our disunity is our destruction.

"'Let us not think like children. In Cacibajagua we lived together and we didn't feel different, and we solved all our problems. But that cave has been erased by the long time we've been in the valley. In this very moment, our lives shorten, our thoughts lengthen, and our souls mortify. We still remember Cacibajagua. What will occur in the days when our minds forget it? Oh Yucahu, how am I to protect my people? Tainos, choose your paths as you have desired, but look at the distance, not always or only at the horizon or at the sky, but all around you and inside you. Thank god, and let us be graceful that Kiskeya is still warmed by the breath of good people.'

"Thus ended the master of Jaragua. All sought their loved ones; they accommodated themselves beside their children, wives, or husbands. They spent the night together, warmed by the heat of the human blood in their body.

The Holy Hill

II

"The birds of the valley, hidden among the green leaves, sing joyfully and take pride with the arrival of the sleepy timid sun. The morning dew still tickles the small children, and everyone feels Bajacu's mild entry. He glides through the fresh air and the foam of the waves of the ocean in the distance, and suddenly the visible clarity of the new day shines; there are huge pieces of sky without threatening, dark clouds, and the gentle sun surprises the path that carries Cibael's tribe; they're heading to his beautiful land. They carry their gods and goddesses in their hands—their royal chief smiles to this and to the lovely day—he knows now that Yucahu accompanies him in his mind—and he feels and sees the god's valuable presence in sight.

"The colorful birds of the valley, now visible, welcome them with their encouraging songs. The trees bend almost touching the ground with the weight of their tropical fruits. The air feels purely fresh, and the terrestrial animals hide with their instinctive fear.

"Cibael and his stronger subjects climb a hill from where La Vega's Royal Valley can be seen completely. Not far away, they find a small plateau. The sky flashes, and thunders roar through the cloudless valley; they take this to be an omen coming from the sacred god. Cibael takes out his Goddess and finds her transformed, dressed in white gold; thunders clash again in the distance. His fellows—now obedient warriors—are shocked by the occurrence and kneel to venerate the powerful royal king. The noble chief is astonished and speechless; he tries to find a thought to convert into words. He declares: 'Oh, Yucahu, master of the sky, where my feet now support the temple of my spirit, here I will build your mother's temple, and this land will be holy to many for centuries; and I will build your house in my house as well.' He promises that much to the god.

"The sky clears, and the common Tainos walk up the Holy Hill and meet the chief and his loyal subjects in the plateau. Clueless of the occurrence, they naturally choose plots where they will build their huts. They see the untested warriors praising the good chief, and as if commanded by the mere god, they imitate the warriors without misgivings.

Somehow they know that Yucahu will live in Cibael's house and will run in the land of Magua, protecting his people; meanwhile Cibael will be as Guatauba, a messenger of the god, or a god of flesh and blood.

"The great chief—jealous of the goddess's statue— hides her in his chest; he turns his back to the believers and shouts that the goddess's temple and his god's house should be made out of pine from the hill. Immediately, the obedient Tainos, men and women, disperse through the hill to chop and collect the best and tallest pine trees and the straws. They begin to build a large hut for the chief. The men carve the pine; the women weave the straws. Rapidly, the formidable, rectangular frame can be admired; it has the casings in the sides for the windows, and the edges of the back and front doors; the inclination of the roof is also visible.

"The green fronds of the palms are used to cover the roof and the sides of the royal hut. Windows are installed simultaneously with the doors, and within hours the shelter looks complete on top of the hill. The Tainos gasp at the wonder they've created, and all gather outside the large shack, which they all call a *caney* to distinguish it from the common huts. Now the chief comes with his disciples, and the crowd gasps at the sight of the goddess that is coming in with the chief. She shines brilliantly and they all kneel at her presence. Once at the door, the royal chief impedes his guardians from entering the hut; he is the only one he trusts with the image.

Once inside, he buries the real Guacar in the center of the *caney*; he brings out an identical fake figurine of the goddess, made from a white Cacibajaguan stone. Then, he opens the door and an altar is brought into the hut by one of his most trusted allies. The chief places the fake goddess on the altar and allows the commoners to come inside the caney to venerate her. After the venerations are finished, the builders hang the hammocks for the chief, his wives, and his children. This completes the construction of the noble chief's house-temple.

"In the next days, they all continue to work ardently, and without noticing it, they build all the necessary huts of the Vegan first small town. A year and two and many fly by as days and unknown spirits are said to wander Magua's borders.

"Guatauba disguises himself as one of Cibael's brothers and meets him in the forest while the chief is sportingly hunting. He is warned: 'Evil and foreign spirits wander your borders. You must secure your boundaries for the protection of your children.' The messenger disappears into thin air with a blink of Cibael's eyes. Cibael feels urgency and runs and calls in a gathering in the *batey*, the ceremonial center of the small town. There he explains the danger of the circumstances. So, he chooses the most loyal and noble people of his tribe, men and women, and he delegates them to every strategic point of his chiefdom; he calls them *Nitainos*. All the Nitainos and fellows novice warriors leave to their appointed sites; they're all

noble in heart; they leave their loved ones behind
for their duties call them; and there are tears in their
eyes, although all of them know that they will stay
within Magua's borders. Each group is carefully
instructed and given strategies. Cibael stands tall
above the crowd and wishes all a triumphantly
return to the Holy Hill.

"Arixis, Cibael's favored son, sets out to explore the
region assigned to him; seven of the stronger and
sprightly Vegans walk through the forest with him.
They crossed the center of the valley together; then
two stay behind until they reach the extreme of the
lovely and seemingly peaceful valley."

(A sudden silence comes from the princess. She
lowers her head, as if she feels a pain in her soul; a
knot is stuck in her throat, and an ancient tear
descends her tender cheek. Although it is a legend
that she tells, she feels affliction as she gathers
herself together to continue telling the story of her
beautiful Kiskeya.

(Anyone could have felt her pain, because then she
spoke of confusion, conflicts, wars and discomforts.

(Now she gathers herself together, lifts her head
vividly and looks into my eyes. Although she is
very sad, because she remembers tragic events, she
continues in this way):

"The Maguans reach the region of *Macorix*–land
within the limits of Cibao; they look like relentless

and fierce warriors, smeared with black from the
charcoal of the previous night firewood ashes;
though they carry green wooden bows and arrows;
those still dressed with their fresh skin. They also
hold huge sharp spears with stone edges. They wear
feather-holding bands on their heads; and
occasionally, they emit a war song that comes out of
their throats in unison; it is a sudden song that
frightens the birds, alerts the mind and any passive
restless spirit; it keeps them away from boredom; at
least that is their intention.

"Someone or something in the universe has invoked
the undesirable *zemi* of war; his reviled presence
infects the air in Macorix; it feels undetainable;
instead it alerts and pushes the bellicose desire
within the native people of Macorix—a tribe more
passive than that of the Tainos themselves—a group
that has never experienced a war. A human howl is
first heard within the disguised passive forest; then
another and another and another; it is a signal of
danger for the Macorixians; a transmission that
escalates to a tremendous rumble, coming from the
Ciguayos—the native people of Macorix. A fury
runs through their veins. A fury that transmits the
hatred through the air; the enemies feel threatened
by the hidden people of this forest. All the
Ciguayans want to release their anger to feel human
once again. The innocent Tainos are frightened;
they don't see anyone in the path ahead or behind
them; it is because the heart-broken people are
hiding within the bushes, or are camouflaged with

the tall thick grass of the forest, or the trees of mango; they are camouflaged as pineapples that crawl on the floor; there are hidden agile Ciguayans everywhere.

"Itahura—famous for his speed in the Vegan village—runs, confused, he runs forward to encounter his enemies and he sees no one. He returns to his four brave companions, then he runs to the back and doesn't even see a trace of his two comrades, who are properly hiding as instructed by Cibael in case of eminent danger. Arixis and Itahura now walk onward carefully and the other three Tainos follow them walking backward, fearfully; their eyes are very alert and active. Arixis is desperate and speaks to the wind: 'Where does your sound come from, wind? Why don't you present yourself to us? We're good people.' The wind returns angry words—undoubtedly made by humans—but Arixis doesn't understand their strange language. The sound, the howl, created with the air and the palm of the hand, repeats itself as a hummingbird's movements; a hungry bird suspended drinking from a flower full of nectar; it is an echo that magnifies three hundred times to alert the people of an eminent danger, indicating a sure war; it maddens and tortures the unfortunate Tainos. Suddenly, a deadly arrow comes from somewhere and cuts through the air; it impacts Itahura—now betrayed by the instinct of his swiftness. An arrow lacerates his temple and another arrow lands on his forehead, splitting his cranium into two equal hemispheres. His body drops instantly to the bitter lifeless surface.

"Arixis, panting, runs to help the exhausted and faithful Itahura. He doesn't find life in him; he sees the clots of blood of his left temple. Suddenly, he sees a spear coming and waving through the air; it looks difficult to dodge; he rapidly moves to his left and stands ready to escape from another lance that comes from his right.

"Now, the fast and strong sound of a coordinated ambush comes from all sides. There is no escape. A spear lacerates Riyamuy's flesh and reaches his heart. He was one of the few men that went by himself in the forest at night and returned safely from the darkness; but now he can't even feel the pain of the sharp-pointed spear that invades and defeats quickly his heart. He kneels on the ground and tries to pull the lance out of his chest; he pulls with all his strength; his soul escapes and his body feels the relief from pain inherited when it is suffering unjustly. His eyes yield and his bust, led by his head, falls to the ground.

"It is now Lineri's turn—the climber of tall trees. Ten angry Ciguayans pursue him; he runs to his left; he runs to his right; he slides through the legs of one of them and escapes. It's like the pursuit of a pack of fierce dogs after an agile cat: the frightened cat runs quickly, but when the feline is cornered and has no escape, he puffs up his hair and fiercely faces his enemies; he always looks for a way to

escape death. The cat is ready to defend himself,
and then he uses his agility; he charges and sprints
towards them; he lands and utilizes their bodies,
bouncing from one to the other to catapult himself
onto the trunk of a tall tree; so does Lineri. Then he
crawls into the branches, fear returns to his soul,
and he hides among the green leaves. The fervent
dogs bark loudly at him, and he trembles with fear,
terrified, nervous, and feeling vulnerable.

"After the climax of their rage arrives, even rabid
dogs calm down and stop their barking; they would
leave and they would forget. But now the
Ciguayans do not feel like dogs, their anger goes
beyond an animal's—they're humans. They leave,
but they come back with stones in their hands; fatal
stones. One of those stones slashes away some of
the green leaves; the enemy is now visible. Another
stone hits him on his strong chest, but he is able to
hold on to a branch; another stone paints him a
purple eye, and down the enemy comes. He drops
like a ripe *soursop* on the ground and the heavy fall
shatters the bones of his extremities. Once
dismembered inside, with little life, sleepy eyes, he
hears the last savage barks of the wild Ciguayans.
But another stone flies and hits him on his right ear;
the sharp sound disappears. Finally, a rain of stones
drops on his body, and life is no more. A man
approaches the dead and twists his head to ensure
that he is without life. In that way, Lineri, once
loved, once useful, ends his odyssey.

28

"Now, the crystalline Ciguayan's victory is at hand; half of the revenge gained; half of the hatred downloaded; but they now have a half light spirit and an intermittent sorrowful soul, because now they know their capacity for violence and their rejection of it; their only protection for existence. Yet, the climax of the chaos lingers in the air. A crowd of late-coming Ciguayans is heard nearby; among the people, there's an inane spirit, a person consumed by a justified hatred of her enemies; infected by sorrow and pain. She is a woman whose soul has been shattered and she can't put herself together because she has lost her only child forever; she is torn by an inner cry that has no compassion; although she is no demon. She is rather possessed by something similar or worse than the impulse of a mother-wolf who has just encountered a hungry beast devouring her only cub in her own den, or as the courage of a lioness that has left her den and when she returns she sees her only cub in the hands of a hunter of fragile prey; her speed and fury are instinctive; she is unable to control her tight nerves, and her revenge surges and looks for destruction based on her hasty suspicion. But, this is a woman who is young, her spirit battered by misfortune, and forgiveness and reasoning are not options in her life; she is maddened by the loss of a son who was slaughtered and roasted like a pig, inserted by a log. Such fury is within this Ciguayan woman. She runs madly toward a Taino man, Bairacoel, who happens to be held by the harsh grip of two Ciguayan hands. The woman gets closer, crying and pushing everyone out of her way. She has a scalpel made out of stone in her hand. She jumps on Bairacoel.

"The woman pries off her co-agent and frees the man from the grip of the Ciguayans; suddenly he feels a sharp knife entering his throat; an abundant torrent of hot blood comes out and splashes her pained faced. She twists the knife and lacerates his flesh as she pulls it out. Then, she stabs the scalpel in his chest with all strength. She falls on top of the bloody corpse and slits his chest. She digs until she finds his heart, still shaking at little; she detaches it from his body and then pulls out his guts and his organs. Now she looks at the sky, holding all her useless possessions, and finally she screams and faints on top of the poor body of the innocent Taino. "Arixis has experienced the bloody act while dodging spears and arrows. His fight is defensive and agile; no Ciguayan has even scratched him yet, protected by the god of war, there isn't a Ciguayan that can hurt him. But soon the mass of Ciguayans surrounds him, and he is now much more than cornered—arrows, spears, and stones aiming at him. They decide to challenge him first. One of them sprints towards him and Arixis receives him with a tremendous immortal punch that makes him fly back to the enemies. Then, impossibility happens and Yucahu appears in the center of the circle, next to Arixis. Nobody else can see him. (Arixis was taught that Yucahu was invisible to humans.) He blinks and the image goes away. A rain of arrows and spears approaches him, he squats on the ground with his head down, waiting for death, but then he gets up, and miraculously Arixis is able to evade them all. The Ciguayans have no more arrows and no more spears. All are astounded. Arixis stands tall now, looking at the heavens. He grabs two spears and aims one of them at the highest ranking member of the tribe present; he now has the opportunity to eliminate at least a few people of the tribe; an opportunity given to him by the god of life.

"Now they reason a little: they have seen that Arixis sought ways to defend himself without malice. (How many Ciguayans would have died if this simple man would have come from a bitter race?)

"Arixis shows them more of himself. He puts the weapons down and collects and makes a bundle with the lances. He carries the sticks on his arms and walks the radius of the circle and drops them on their feet. He returns for the arrows with tears in his eyes and pain in his chest; nothing can counsel him; he cries the deaths of his comrades. He picks up all the pointed sticks and throws them angrily at the Ciguayans. He returns to the center angrier than before and screams furiously the names of Bairacoel, Riyamuy, Lineri, and Itahura. Exhausted, he throws himself on the ground, in the middle of the Ciguayan crowd, ready to give them his life. He bows and lowers his head; he gives them a perfect target for the arrows and the spears. But now, the king of miracles, Yucahu himself, invisible to all, calms down the Ciguayan spirits even more, and they all return to the level of a holy compassion. A huge silence spreads through all the forest; but it is

merely temporary because one of the two hiding
Tainos cannot stand the pain in his chest and he
sighs loudly. He is full of valor and anger and his
commoved spirit pushes him toward the Ciguayans;
he cannot allow them to kill so cowardly his friend.
But that is not his task, so his companion grabs him
by the arm and reminds him of it. They can only
imagine what will happen to Arixis. They gather
themselves together and begin their journey to their
far land in the Holy Hill, but not without contention.

"The Ciguayans become active again, but don't
hold the disgusting revenge in their hearts; they are
rather fearful and dubious of their action. Twenty of
the most agile men run armless after the innocent
poor accomplices. They have left all the arrows and
lances on the ground, around Arixis. They run
quickly and lightly in spirit because they don't carry
the vindictive hatred in their veins. But the Tainos
are faster, afraid, with an important task at hand;
their escape to save their people. One of them trips
on a small rock; he falls to the ground and skins his
left knee; he rises and limps. His friend cannot leave
him behind, so he suddenly stops and the halt makes
him wobble. He goes back and assists his friend
whose fear makes him well in a hurry. They get to a
place where the tall grass and the entangled trees
give hope to the escapees; it has never been touched
by man. They run into the tall grasses together and
they seem to have lost them among the wild maize;
they continue dodging tress and all obstacles that
meet their way. Finally, when they feel safe, they
stop. Then, they look ahead and see a moderate

cliff; they hear Ciguayan voices and their hope is gone again.

"The panting Ciguayans arrive and block the innocent Tainos. The fugitives look at each other; they are at a loss; they find themselves between the grip of angry people and the cliff, but they have no idea what is down that precipice. Resolved, they run towards the abyss, jump and find out that the cliff is not as steep as they have thought, but it is still rough. So they roll and roll down the ravine, always protecting their faces as they coil and unwind, stand and stagger again, rolling from side to side until they hit the bottom alive, dizzy, battered and without any strength left. They look up and no Ciguayan dares to do the same; they are not as bold or perhaps they don't need to risk as much. But soon the Tainos find out that they are relentless; down come climbing the bold Ciguayans. The Tainos look at themselves in the faces again; then they look ahead and sigh because they see a hope of an escape again.

"They see the river Yuna up ahead, its flow contrary to their destination. The current is menacing; its waterway is utterly full. There's no place to hide and the Ciguayans are just a few steps within reach. They would not contend well on even ground with those ferocious beasts of this forest. So Yucahu pushes them little by little toward the water; he gives them valor until they sprint toward the water like hungry leopards towards their prey; although, they are now the targeted prey.

"(Oh, if only they had realized that Yucahu had also softened their enemies' stony bitter hearts!)

"They get to the edge of the bank and dive into the fury of the water. Yucahu is with them; they swim and breathe under the water as fish in the ocean. The current is rough and unyielding, but Yucahu pushes them across to the other side of the river. But caution demands from them ardent work as they crawl like snakes out of the river into tall grasses. When they feel safe in the other side, they stand still sore and afraid. They make sure that nobody follows them; only they could have been so intrepid.

"Their journey is long and uncertain, but the urgency gives them anxiety and the nerves give them the precise reason. Their families are safe for now in the distance, but not thousands or three hundred thousand leagues away from this horrible location; they had gotten here fairly quick themselves. So, their enemies can reach their village as well. The trauma of the horror, the slaughter of their comrades, and the why of the moment torment their minds; all that matters is the hope of surviving, of warning and protecting their loved ones; they can't do anything about their dead loved ones; they died under the pressure of something more evil than revenge or maybe revenge itself. This wretched spirit, friend to hatred, cannot come to their village, home to brothers and sisters. What excuse will they give to their parents and the most vulnerable? True warning, when evil is possible, is such a blessing!

They reason and remember their royal chief. They were told to travel behind as a precaution, for they did not know what world they were sent to explore. Protection hints at an evil thing. That's the reason why Cibael had told them not to abandon caution to go after unnecessary little social pleasures. They did well, or so they feel.

"Their conversation tunes about Cibael's warnings and advices. After failure on a task, responsibility can be taken off a man's shoulder, but the mind weakens and honor is forfeited for the person does not deserve it or merit it. But they have caused no failure yet, their task is to get to the village to tell the unfortunate event, befallen to their comrades. But for that they have to find luck. And luck, the compassionate, was the cause of the smile that Cibael showed when he dispatched them to the wilderness. He told them that she was part of his god, Yucahu. The good luck or pleasant thing unexpected would not abandon them, and it would return them home full of hope and their spirits, without a doubt, would rejoice because they would get to a safe sanctuary where the presence of Yucahu they would peacefully feel.

"(O, how much their hearts wish to be next to Cibael, the most merciful, the great commander and demander!)

"In the distance, almost at dusk, panting like wild dogs without destination, they stop and take refuge under a small multicolored tree; they feel safe and

35

sit down to chat before they go to sleep. They remember Cibael's predictive words. They had listened to feel encouraged:

"'Stay behind and hide to survive if necessary. You are the people or the descendants who are or will be Nitainos. If a misfortune occurs to your peers and Yucahu is with you, luck, too. Yucahu is life and hope; if you are alive at any time or at any moment, so is Yucahu. If luck is not with you, ask Yucahu fearlessly because he is the mere fountain of it. If you feel lost, without the strength to live, think of the fate that is short-sighted, and she will give you the courage you need. Luck is eternal in our village, or so it seems. Here a child runs freely, plays happily, jokes joyfully, and laughs without fear. A man shares his fishing gains, a woman her harvesting, and all the skills of survival and services are common. It may not be good luck, but luck it is.

"'You are free to ask Yucahu whatever you wish, or ignore or deny what you want without societal pressure. Everybody here has his or her importance. Equality is well distributed among the common people. A good fisherman builds a simple hut at will, and the cultivator of fruits builds the same; a simple hut is what the novice artisan possesses. We celebrate life at night together. Isn't that luck?

"'The nights full of stars illuminate our village. Here we dance with peace as our companion, we thank nature for our existence, and we differentiate the personal from the mythical stories. Men and women are certainly respected. Here, misfortunes are opaque when compared to the clarity of our satisfactions. That and more is the set of things that we should call luck. We live in peace. What is more pleasant than peace and social justice? To live in peace is the luck of the living. Oh, woe to those who wish for more than a family, a hut, a little cassava, and a society who lives in the present and is a hater of war.' So the comrades remember.

"So the night comes and sleep closes their eyes and the bitter anguish opens them as they wake up from a vivid dream, and their weariness makes them fall back into a deep sleep and anguish again awakens in them concerns of an unquiet soul. But then they think of Yucahu, as Cibael had suggested them, and they calm down and evade all those things that torment them, and they gather their spiritual strength and with faith they find rest in their sleep.

"At dawn Bajacu glides through the leaves of the trees, shaking gently the branches where the birds and the small reptiles rest. On the ground, lizards and iguanas walk like holding hands, in love with their partners. A humming bird zooms by the ear of one of the comrades and he awakens. A snake, as large as an arm, hisses and eats insects next to the sleeping companion. His comrade picks up his bow and an arrow which he inexplicably still possesses. The armed Taino cautiously steps back from the action with the intention to do nothing. The threatening looking snake navigates on the sleeping

Taino's chest, and naturally he feels something. He wakes up calmly and when he sees the snake, he grabs her before she throws at him her harmless bite. Immediately, he hears laughter from his dear friend who was waiting for the snake to strike him. "He doesn't do this as a villain for the joke was an ingenuity of nature; fear and worry were none. No evil unfolds upon his fellow; it is all a sane trick intended; his land is or was a paradise. The snake could have bitten his companion, but she wouldn't have affected the presence of Yucahu; there is no poison in the snakes of this land. They're as gentle as the good people of this land—Tainos—that exist here by the lot.

"Nonetheless, the game goes on. Revenge looks terrible even as imitation. The fellow gets up and curves the snake as a pet around his neck. Then he goes quickly after his friend, imitating fury itself and the rapidity of a demon; but he is a man disguised as a saint, with his fangs hidden, and his claws behind his back; his demonic plan well defined. The moment is trapped in the imagination of deception; it is indeed far from the truth. The snake hisses on his neck as he approaches his comrade. His friend still laughs and is ready to run away. But the companion shouts from the short distance that the game should be over for they have to continue their journey. The playful friend kneels on the ground and asks for forgiveness, and it is granted. He gets up and hugs his friend, but his friend quickly grabs him and wrestles him down; fangs and claws out; he takes out his illusory knife and stabs his companion a hundred times. The demon sees the fellow agonizing on the ground and laughs as loud as he can. Blood and misery are parts of the imitation. The demon deposes the excruciating man of all his valuable possessions, places the harmless snake on the ground, next to the companion, and runs like a man toward his loved ones.

"So, they play during the day and sleep at night until they get safely to their village. As they walk along the road to the Holy Hill, the artisans stop their work to observe them; the women come out of their huts, a gossip of their misfortune spreads from neighbor to neighbor, and fear and uncertainty conquer many hearts at once. Cibael receives them with hugs and curiosity. A pain runs through their souls. They are glad to arrive home, but the message they carry torments them as they remember the faces of the worried women and the hopeless men as they entered the batey and the images of the comrades with defeated forms. They are lead into the *caney* and into a private room within it. They are frightened and speechless in the presence of the king. He hastens them to talk for uncertainty can easily kill a chief and they carry the truth.

"One of them takes the lead: 'Luck and good luck are less gracious than what your presence bestows upon me, my chief. But terrible and unpleasant are the images that luck allowed me to see. First, the songs of the new warriors traveled with us from the beginning of our journey; and you are a witness to this. The birds of the valley sang to us a lullaby, and I confess that only once we betrayed a sage's advice, and for that reason two of us still stand well and alive before you; we spent one night together and heard our comrades enjoy each other's talks as we suffered their alienation after that, as you had commanded. We stayed behind a fair distance and kept our watch as you had commanded the night before our happy departure. But deep within the forest, we heard wary cries of savages. I wanted to run to meet my comrades and death itself. My companion's patience stopped me once and twice and thrice; he held me again and again and reminded me of my noble task. If patience is a virtue, my chief, a patient action is an extreme; we hid under a bush long-sufferingly, as evil unfolded within the road of misfortune; I dare to say that we are alive and therefore lucky. But I cannot say the same about our warriors, and because of their misfortune, I felt myself a coward. Confusion took hold of my mind. Savage cries can give a sane man nothing but impatience. I had an eye to detect danger; when the first mortal arrow came, I saw it coming slowly, though nothing could have traveled so quickly. I sprinted from my hiding bush, and landed shortly on my belly; exposure could not travel far. My companion, here present, grabbed me roughly by the waist, wrestled me down, kept my peevish head on the dirt, and quieted me down. I lifted my head and saw when the arrow stroked the brave and swift Itahura on his left temple. Hopelessness defeated me once. I felt I could have saved him once; but death would have come to two instead. My friend dragged me into the densely leafed-bush and the darkness concealed us from danger, but I looked through a breach of light and another arrow cracked the dead's cranium. I screamed as if it had impacted me and my painful outcry passed undetected for madness had spread thoroughly in this portion of the forest. O, my chief, I can't bear to remember how anger took possession of my mind. To see Riyamuy liberate his soul from suffering as he pulled a lance out of his heart is a stab in a brother's heart. I could not resist the pain no more. But my companion begged me to calm down and to listen to reason as our chief adviser. Lineri was chased by a crowd of angry and savage beasts. He died most unjustly. I swallowed pain and sorrow and injustice. I do not have the strength or courage to recount the misfortune befallen to Bairacoel; the face of horror is the description of the event. I was motionless and voiceless as it happened. But soon I am slapped by the madness. The whole crowd was after the bravest of the pack, Arixis. I could not allow my eyes to see no more. I sprinted again out of the bush and wished to defend him or die fighting the savages with him. But my friend detained me once again. I struggled though, and I beseeched my mind for impatient action. We argued briefly and he told me to take hold of patience for she is a noble being, and therefore I was not a weakling as I thought. I unwillingly stepped out of my hiding place; Arixis was a captive and a prey of the savages. I thought of the

village and thought of Arixis. I could not save
Arixis nor did I think I could then save myself. But
the voice of my companion begged me to run, not
for my sake, but for the sake of a treasurable
village. We left Arixis on the verge of death. Our
standing here is a cause of luck, my chief.' So the
comrade finishes.

"Cibael feels the pain and asks the companion:
'What do you have to add to this?' Silence sings a
dirge in reply to the chief. His voice is muted and
anger destroys him from within. His blood boils and
sweat or fever reddens his face and his watery eyes;
tears flow out of his eyes and pain takes his dire
form. Fear and anger melt into one and the man
shakes like a volcano about to explode; his body is
weak and trembling defeats him quickly; the sight is
painful. Injustice and despondency force him to
kneel on safe refuge. The royal chief approaches
him, gives him a soothing hug, and thanks him for
his honorable reply. All is said. The stricken royal
chief screams like a ravenous-for-revenge and
maddened man; all he has heard or seen possesses
many descriptions or details but everything sounds
wrong or seems unpleasant to the soul. He puts his
hands on his reasonable and patient head, and
distress and pain speak most eloquently. But the
chief frightens off the evils and his valor makes him
reign again with clever patience. His valor shows
well in his cautious decision. Reason calls his mind
to an urgent conference together with his most
trusted people. The rumors that Cibael is not feeling
well and that the painful clamor brought by his

loyal soldiers riots in his chest bruit about the
village. The astute man demands patience.
"But within the village, the worried men stop
working, silence keeps the small children in check,
and weeping mothers lament their children's deaths
with the unconfirmed gossip. The council is
besieged by the newfangled predicament. The
entanglement consumes hours after hours of
unfruitful reasoning. The councilmen disbelieve
what they have heard and find no words to appease
the chief's discontent. A rumor finds his way to
Cibael's ear and this makes the situation even
worse: the women and the children are afraid; evil
spirits are said to roam the darkest forest. The
advisers agree that a decision should be made in
haste. Cibael addresses them angrily: 'Do you think
me a fool? What decision would it be? To tell them
their assumptions are true and deprive hope of its
enrichment. Don't be foolish! Give these warriors
crystal water from my jug, give them fresh food
from my table, and let them relax in the hammocks
of my own hollow. As for you, hasten out of my hut
and pretend to live your lives with normality. Let
assumption take hold of people's hearts, for
supposition can give a person false hope and keep
them happy for a while. Evade all comments about
the matter and tomorrow when all seem to be
confirmed, we will tell them that we have lost a
meaningless battle with men of wicked spirits; and
it shall be the truth, if the truth has been spoken by
the lips of honest and courageous men. Do not
besmirch their effort for it would certainly make of
you cowards. Be gone now.'

"The councilmen are poked with a sword of anger, and the scolding does not make them obedient to the cause. Outside the hut, these men and women quarrel among themselves; some in favor of Cibael's decision, and some in opposition. One of them says: 'What is the purpose of a court, if qualified opinions are not heard? Some of you say that the chief has never been wrong, and that virtue is his crown. But, think of the people. When has such a common crowd reasoned out of virtue? Tell them the truth; a group of mad people have killed our loved friends, our sons, and our cousins; and they will want revenge, and still they will seek a lie to quench unwanted fear. Tell the people that evil spirits killed our friends and kin, and they will hide with fear, and an unnecessary war would be won without throwing a spear.' Nothing else is said and as ordered by the king, they keep their anguish in secrecy, or so they make believe.

"Rumor wakes up from a nap and multiplies like meiosis; it bruits about the suspicious village; it carries half the truth and half invention, as if a mouth can't ever repeat exact words; or as if the ear always receives befitting benefits. Spirits abound in the forest and evil men callously murder mercy and conceive unstoppable revenge and continual hatred. That's the rumor. A war is imminent if survival is a priority; the rumor creates a reverse reaction.

"The night falls on the village like a heavy burden on a fragile soul. Cibael's beloved wife stands at a corner of the caney; she hasn't spoken a word since the comrades had arrived. She weeps in silent and a sudden scream comes from within her: 'He's alive! He cannot be dead!' She says and faints as the ground receives her gently. The maids assist her quickly and a rumor runs out of the caney and creates a commotion out of nerves on all the women; some scream hysterically because they have a missing son and some scream in support or out of fear or orchestrated by a councilwoman who believes that a single man cannot carry on his shoulder an entire nation, nor can a nation be commanded by a single man.

"But Cibael knows all thoughts of his nation; he is a brilliant man of a learned spirit; he has inclined his mind toward war, but his main god has detained him from making a hastened decision, regardless of the contrived reaction of rioted spirits. So he quickly calls back into the caney his main trusted men and women, and beseeches them to find a cure to the uproarious acts of masked desperation; and he orders some to console the truly heartbroken mothers and fathers and to ask them for justifiable patience. The mothers of those who died do not listen to reason or motive for the peaceful delay; the gossips and their instinctive prefiguration assure them of the barbarous acts they have heard. So, the ground cannot contain them; the pain in their chests moves them from side to side; their souls want to come out of their flesh, but nature can only call a soul a prisoner; the women show their motherly pain vividly.

"Cibael realizes that he needs to play a harsh game; he has never seen an evil manifesting so boldly and criminally. So, he makes a decision: a demon does not like the truth. He calls on his Behique, the main priest and healer of his village. He is taken to the back of the caney and Cibael awaits him there. He bows to the floor and the great chief tells him: 'Stand up and act as if you were my equal for I must trust in you. How can a man trust an unequal, or an unequal a man? It is a dangerous enterprise of cultural value that I will put on your hand, and I do not know if it is a perpetual malice, but I think that the moment deserves its merit. I just hope it evaporates as quick as it came to my head, or it will be like ropes on our necks. Are you up for the task?

"The Behique says: 'How can a man reject such an honor, my chief? But I do not know the details of the trick, and yet I feel compelled to agree, not by your cautious words, but by the merit that you speak of.'

"The chief replies: 'I do agree. Your task, the why, and the details are all entangled in these human dealings: My task, immense as the house of the stars, or as little as Magua, is to provide protection to my people; to keep our ways of live is my pride; and to help Maguans grow like fruitful seeds, now under hardened soil, attacked by worms and mental parasites, cannot be more than a challenge; my task is as immense as the soul of my God, for it could perish if the infection extends to all of Kiskeya. I am well-informed about the good people of

Kiskeya. Few of them know that the Macorixians, as passive as they are, could be threatened, if they are not already dead, by the savage Caribs. Certainly, my eyes weren't witnesses to the slaughter of our warriors, but I assume that the Caribs were the worms of the discomfort. If they wander in such numbers in our valley, as I think it is reported by my men, they will attack the heart of our village, our Holy Hill, and a part of Kiskeya will be rotten. A body cannot allow a part of it to rot, for it could soon consume the whole; Kiskeya should be aware of the infection, and together the Kiskeyans must find a responsible cure.

"'Within my village, there's a councilwoman, an instigator, who wants to keep us from going to war; reasoning that we will be better protected by securing our village and not parting away to a far, uncontrolled, and unknown land. Yet, another woman wants immediate revenge and thinks that we should hasten into the dangerous forest. I've been told that you're a trusted man, a healer of discomforts and a learned man in the ways of men and women. I'll share with you a cure; inject it to quench the women's pains; for a demon devours them from within; it was created by the lies of gossips and contrived fear.

"'Tell them the contrary to my belief. I think that when a person dies, his or her spirit vanish from existence; it does not suffer or walk aimlessly in a dark or lit heavenly place as some want to believe;

47

but this is promising. Tell the women about Coaybay, a lost land in a cave under the earth where spirits don't suffer nor do they walk aimlessly or want to come back to earth; that's where their sons' spirits are and will stay there for eternity. Or create yourself a better story. Include in it Maketaori Guayava, the strictest guardian in the universe, and the overseer of Coaybay. Tell them that his passion cannot be equaled and that it is the mere essence of his laborious existence. Also, tell them that Maketaori Guayava does not feel the love of a good father or that of a good mother for every spirit is judged blindly; injustice has no place there; and that evil has no place like it has in some places on earth. Let the lie come closer to the truth so that it doesn't hurt us harshly someday. I am sad to know a seeming truth: common people would rather hear a falsehood that would give them hope and the supposition of eternity than hear the truth that would give them pain and with time immune them and cure them slowly. Do your task and gain loyalty; orchestrate tomorrow night festivities and tell the people that I will address them, and your success will be rewarded with my trust.'

"The Behique is elevated. He goes on to deliver the medicine; and this reduces the women's pains. The men are happy with the change and support the Behique. Cibael sends a spy for supervision. She hears the Behique as he is saying: '. . . There are no sufferings there, there are no feelings, nor does a soul lives like a soul lives within a person on earth. I believe that nobody wants to be there, but some day we will visit the land of non-existence. So, people must not suffer to the point of hurting themselves for the loss of a kin. Stay alive and reason well for there's nothing for those who arrive at the dark door of Maketaori Guayava. I assure you that those that kill your sons committed a big error. They don't think well, they suffer a lot, but they live here on earth. We should not think like them. We should think well, make the fewest mistakes of the soul, and live happily and peacefully on earth.'

"So, the healer does as his chief has commanded. He becomes a great imitator; he keeps his feelings in the deepest part of his soul, and he brings them out when he desires. He does not waste his time and quickly uses the liberated women to help him gather a crowd in the *batey*. He tells the people that at night there would be smoking, illustrations, dances, commemorative talks, and prayers for the god and goddess. The message spreads to every ear on the village. The sun rises on the horizon and the children can be seen with their father's maracas; some inspect the *güiras*, and some men and women even try on their masks. The behique gathers a group of boys and girls; he gives to each a role; he describes them their performing actions; he recites to them all the words; he shows them the steps of the dances; and he begs them to practice all of these to perfection.

Macorix: Caribs Raid

III

"Back in Macorix, the day of the chase is intact, but it now moves as the chasing Ciguayans return without their prey. The Tainos have escaped. Panting, afraid, and angry the Ciguayans arrive at the menacing chanting circle. Arixis has not been hurt physically yet; but the Ciguayans torment him with a Macorixian's chant that translates into: 'Who are you? Why are you here? Are you a demon?' Arixis's head is fixed on the ground, his strong hands are crossed on his back, and his thoughts are lost in oblivion. The Taino rises brusquely with the lift of a quasi-friendly hand. Then, he stands fearlessly and walks with a chief that sustains his arm as if he was a terrible, bitter, impious, and dangerous prisoner; the chanting crowd follows him.

"On the way to the center of the town, two racks over an extinguished fire hold the suspended skeletons of two roasted children. A white dirty fresh powder with strips of black particles on the ground is evidence that a celebration with a BBQ infected the forest one, two or three moons ago. Arixis scans the site and the countenances of the people, and he cannot see anything more than sadness. He walks gently with the inconsolable chief, and the crowd behind, and as they pass the site, Arixis finds himself being dragged on the rough ground of the hellish-feeling forest. His lips bounce on small rocks and dirt mingles with hot blood; his knees peel as he sweeps the ground and his mind's eye flashbacks to images of his comrades' misfortune.

"Soon, the throng arrives at the center of their town and immediately they construct a frame, two triangles connected with a center stick, and underneath it they prepare the sticks for the bonfire. Now Arixis realizes their cruel intention. He sighs deeply and someone reties his innocent hands and his feet together, behind his back. Then, they throw him near the frame as if he were a pig, ready to be roasted. Some youngsters chant; some women squat on the ground showing bitter pains; and some men delay the procedure for they don't have the authority from the main chief. But waiting is not a pain-killer, so someone inserts the center stick through Arixis's extremities and a force lifts him up and fixes him on the rack. Arixis tries to extricate himself from the knot. He gives up. Instead he shouts: 'Have you no hearts? Why are you going to burn me alive? Adopt a human feeling! Propel a mortal arrow on to my head or crack the space between my eyes with a sharp stony spear. But don't pretend to seek a noble satisfaction out of a cruelty.' Nobody understands his pleading language. Instead, an old man approaches the unfortunate soul—half-hidden soul within Arixis's temple. The man takes a rope, grabs Arixis's hair and stabs a spear on Arixis's ribs; Arixis opens his mouth with a painful cry, and the old man ties a knot in Arixis's mouth.

"But a woman approaches the old man and says: 'Why? Didn't he find pleasure at the expense of an innocent child? Liberate the filthy mouth of the swine and let it squeak until the fire dries all the substance of his soul. Let it squeak now, and when the fire is on, let him scream with a longer painful aaaaaaah! He deserves no better.' She unties the knot. Arixis sighs. Though he thinks that he has found mercy, but as quickly as he is slapped by the woman, he sees in her eyes the terrible look of anger.

"A man sparks two stones and the friction creates the wanted strange soul of fire and a stick is soon with a flame. The man blows on the bundle of sticks underneath Arixis and Arixis exclaims: 'Why! Why! Are you savages also insane? Do you pretend to eat me? What kind of animals are you? Man should not eat man! Not even the lowest of animals consider such measures; a dog does not eat a dog;

nor does the shark a shark, or the monkey a
monkey. Although you don't understand my words,
your eyes cannot be so blind, I don't ask for mercy,
eat me if you want, but don't be cowards and kill
me with a knife as you would kill a pig. Oh,
Yucahu, master of the good men, why do you teach
me such unkind things the minutes before my
death? Where do these savage animals, capable of
reasoning, find a satisfaction unknown to me? Oh,
my nature, have mercy on them, for they are
without knowledge and know nothing of justice!'
"The royal Ciguayan chief comes out of the caney
and lays his eyes on Arixis for the first time from
the distance; the crowd opens up like a curtain; they
create a space, a clear path for the main chief, and
they also prostrate themselves to venerate his
presence; a behique and two guardians follow the
steps of the kingly chief. The cacique is trilingual
and Taino is one of his studied languages. He has
examined the compass of the prey's language from
the distance: 'Put up the fire quickly', he commands
in his own language. 'This man is not a Cariban.
Have you sense of his language, you would have
noticed that he talks about nature and justice: two
foreign concepts for the members of the Cariban
tribe; this man is a Kiskeyan and I think that we
have mistakenly killed his brothers. He and his
people probably, I am now certain, have nothing to
do with the evil befallen on our village. Untie him
and let him stand on firm ground; I will address him
now.' The royal chief changes his tongue; now he
speaks Taino: 'Before I apologize for an injustice,

tell me, do you have anything to do with the calamity befallen on my village?'

"The Taino says: 'No, my chief, I know nothing of it.' He feels some relief because he understands the simple question; so he continues: 'You don't have to apologize for anything. Instead, I beseech you to have mercy on me and protect me from insane feelings; and god will make you lucky.'

"The kind chief replies: 'So, it should be granted. Tell me your origin and give a name to your father.'

"'First, my noble chief, allow me to thank for your kindness. My own name is Arixis and I am from Magua, the land of my father Cibael.' The cacique, the behique, and the highest ranking nobility gasp at the news.

"The chief says: 'Then, I must apologize for my people. There shouldn't have to be a justification for insanity and cowardice, but I assure you that those evils have nothing to do with the attack experienced unjustly by your people. We are not cowards here nor are we insane. So please, listen to the injustice brought to my town by true cowards and insane people. Then, judge us accordingly. You are my guest now.'

"The great chief commands the roasting of snakes and birds instead. A princess meets the hurting man; she guides him swiftly into the caney and with crystal water removes dirt from the swollen cuts in his lips and purple cheeks and broken nose. A few maids join her and they clean his body and apply a curing paste and a scented ointment. His sparkling eyes revive and scan the princess's body and perceive a mutual predetermined romantic feeling. Then, she brings him cassava, juice, and a piece of roasted snake and a small bird. Arixis can barely move his shattered lips and he eats the delicious food slowly; the noble princess comes and helps him. They smile and laugh and chat, and this thing called love does its magic unconsciously.

"Outside the *caney*, a vital conference, among the royal chief, the *behique*, and the elders, spurs a debate about a living prophecy in which someday a mighty prince will enter the *Ciguayan* town, tied and heartbroken, maltreated and agonizing; but he will rise again and the cause of his dealings will bring vengeful destruction and subordination to the peaceful town. One of the elders warns the royal chief. And the chief says: 'I know the content of the omen, but I never wanted to hear the details from my father. What is the origin of it? Am I to become fearful or rather cautious?'

"An elder replies: 'Indeed, my chief, both.'

"And the chief: 'Illustrate me with the origin?'

"The elder answers: 'I will, my chief. A Cacibajaguan priest came down from *Cauta* and fell in love with this land of ours. He was a true dreamer and all his divinations made our people believers under the heaven. He predicted the darkening of a day, and it was so. Thousands of guesses he made came true. He returned to the heart of *Cauta*, took his wife and children, and brought them here to live. One day he jumped out of his hammock and ran to the royal chief on the beach; his agitation brought confusion to the town and the people saw in him a drunkard. He said to them that in three days the gentle sea would act like a demon; it would uproot the toughest trees, the strongest huts would fly in the sky, and fear would reign as a cruel chief. He took his family into a cave and suggested the people to do the same. But the sky was crystal clear, not a single rainy cloud was near. The day before his prediction, he came out of the cave completely nude and begged the people to hide with him in the cave; they called him a drunkard again. And so he told them: <One day, Maguan people will come to your land. They will seem fierce unlike the gentle sea, which maddened, hidden current roars like nothing you have seen; but these people will be gentle in their hearts like the calm sea that you now see. You will destroy many of them for a fault cause but one will survive and his blood will draw conquerors and destruction and subordination to your people; just like the madden sea that you believe to be so gentle.' And in three days, the maddened sea began to roar and lightning illuminated the sky, and thunders rumbled in the deepest part of heaven; the sea's waves were like the fangs of an imagined beast that nips at victims intermittently; and the

flying palm trees and the huts became like flying menace crashing and exploding in the air. The Taino came out of the cave after the destruction. The sea was calm again. So he built a few canoes and he took his family beyond the horizon, claiming that there were islands in the distance. The story has been told for generations even though it was not to the taste of all the former chieftains of this clan. That's the origin of the oracle, my chief.'

"The royal chief does not look convinced: 'What do you say, behique?'

"The behique replies: 'My chief, if we let him leave the village and he comes back with friends and vengeful deeds, a callous prophecy will be fulfilled. Find out if he is of a vengeful kind; recount to him our sad story, and let nature take its course as it ought to be.'

"The royal chief retorts: 'Enough of this imagination. I know his people. This Taino man is now my guest and I will treat him accordingly, as a man of honor. As the saying goes, nature is the best maker and she always aims at perfection. Dismiss, I will meet the Taino now.'

"This laden oracle does not make the chief discomforted, and his soul, unmoved by suppositions, leads him into the caney. The presence of Yucahu is strong within the sacred house. The gracious air purifies the souls with happy laughter and conversations. The soothing mood embraces the chieftain's spirit; he feels relieved from a burden. When the presence of the chief takes a stand, the princess and maids disperse about the caney; some come out immediately; then all of them. The chief addresses his guest: 'Have you ambitions, or vengeful thoughts or feelings, my brother?'

"'No, none at all, my chief,' he says. 'Why do you inquire about such things?'

"'Circumstances, son, circumstances,' says the chief. 'You will have the opportunities to talk about them. Suppositions can undoubtedly create chaos in a religious clan; without the truth we are doomed to fail. But assumptions have nothing to do with the injustice done to you and your companions; my people's revenge emanated from an uncompassionated truth. Injustice is a very bad action, experienced not felt, son; you might notice the pain in the crying of the people; the result of injustice seems to be an incurable lament of the soul. Revenge is the wrong medicine, if it be a medicine at all. It is clemency that cures injustice, for it is an equal action, and not an equal feeling; you can also see the effect taking place in the village. When they saw you and your friends, clemency was not in the mind of any Ciguayan. However, customs or habits show a person clemency, or the soul feels a burden. They saw clemency when I spoke about you and your people, and immediately they offered it to you. It was them who brought you down from the rack and gave you water and food; they are Ciguayans, born with the good custom. Listen carefully.

"'Three days full of sadness were brought here in huge buckets and they were emptied on our humble village. Our hearts are so gentle that we, as a people, forget about the acts of injustice; caution slips through our fingers, but nature has no fault, for it is part of the perfection of humans to err. Everything began with an act of kindness. We saw lost canoes battling the harsh water of the old horizon. These old and tired eyes of mine can accurately distinguish the bubbles of the sharks from those of the whales in the distance; but this time they failed to identify the huge evil intention of the people in those canoes; a fault of mine. Since childhood, my father taught me the details of that water. I saw that any daring person would have no trouble with the even tides of the season; yet my heart was full of goodness for it had experienced no evil in a long time; another fault in me. My father told me about the nature of this island; it was and is and will be an open port for the flowing of all kinds of people; the evil and the wicked, the good and the noble; they will always come and go he said.

"'Those people in those canoes were wicked beings, are you the noble kind? You're a Taino, therefore you must be kind and noble in deed; I can see it in your eyes. The days of my childhood are not forgotten. Naturally, my father taught me Taino, for that was the language of the people who came through from Cauta and left on canoes to other islands. I taught my children, all princes and princesses, the tongue of the Siboney, for those are the people closer to us. I know your nation's heart. But I forgot my wise father's warnings and through a fault of mine I put my people in danger. I know very well that part of the sky; if division is a skill, I know every piece of it. The sky of that horizon, at times, carries heavy loaded clouds, and at times, its clarity creates the blue of the sea. The sharks chose naturally the depth of the water under the horizon as their frontier and the whales give births to their off-springs in our gentle winter, in the water of the bay. The foam in the waves is black as the night and white as cotton. The storms are violent and the rain falls as if from buckets. How could I not know that danger wasn't a factor?

"'Oh, my son! In that mere horizon, disguised as fragile and troubling souls, the wicked Cariban men imitated a fight with mighty nature; they seemed to be looking for something. And as we signaled that help was coming, they quickly disappeared, seeming capable and able to tame the gentle waves, beyond my known horizon. Later, an agonizing man, battered by the waves, half-buried in the white sand, hiding evil as secrecy, attracted pity and commotion. A Macorixian man did all the necessary things to revive him, and he began to breathe slowly and to utter words of appreciation. He found the strength, imitating weakness, to explain the false events of his survival. He fell in the water, swam away from the hungry sharks, and riding on a pitiful crest of nature, he was splashed heavily on the shore. Without any more strength to talk, he fainted on the arms of the supportive Ciguayan. The Macorixian man carried him on his shoulders and took him to his humble hut. There, he cured his wounds and dripped juice in his mouth to feed him. He slept until his fatigue went away. When he awoke, he was given yucca, soursop juice, and a piece of manatee. In late afternoon, he was given maize, honey, and cassava.

"'At night he was already standing on his feet. Oh the scoundrel, the ungraceful soul or spiritless being, as contradicting as it may sound, made inquiries about the start of our working day, the children's games, and our nightly events. Even I invited him to my hut, and gave him all the unobservable details. He learned the contrast between friendship and hostility; he timed our daily festivities, and he examined our caution. He counted the stars and calculated in secret; he concluded all in his favor. The assault would go on as planned.

"'The next day he woke up with the songs of the morning birds. He was a helping hand; he carried the vessels of drinking water for the recent moms; he helped on the gathering of firewood within the near forest; he collected fruits and vegetables from the planted field. He kept some aside for himself hidden in the forest. When he was offered food, he declined the generosity; he was fasting until nighttime. And so the dreadful night came, the people gathered for the bonfire and their story-telling. The villainous soul refuted all invitations and sorrow and afflictions were his excuses and we all understood him, or we were all betrayed by his ingenuity. He claimed that his hunger was annexed by his sheer disconsolation; no food was necessary and nostalgia was his only dilemma. So he walked on to the corner of the beach by himself and there he built a campfire; the sticks were aligned strategically, and when he burned the wood, a white smoke ascended to the sky without much wavering. The evil sign was seen in the distance by the decoders. So the Cariban men invaded the empty beach in four large, rapid, strong and comfy canoes. The scoundrel guided them to a precise location and they captured a child of three months and another of four. Furtively, they disappeared in the dark forest.

"'Within the forest, the evil men found two barbecue racks, built by the scoundrel, ready for the hellish fire. The babies must have cried like pigs. Oh, I can't control my revengeful instinctive nature, and yet I am self-compelled to draw the blue images so retrograde to my nature that I shiver to the mere thoughts of my imagination. They must have stabbed the desperate babies in their hearts to shut them up and to drain their blood as they would drain the blood of a pig. Then, they cut them open and deposed of their beating little hearts, the guts and all their human organs. And if putting condiments, before they roast or bake fish, a pig or a manatee was not in their eating habit, the scoundrel adapted to it quickly, for they left evidence of the seasoning on the bloody rocks, where we found the coagulated blood and organs. They hanged the heads on the logs that served as the columns for the racks; their eyes were still open when we found them. They must have forgotten about the time or about the caring nature of parents for even before we had finished our nightly gathering at the campfire, we heard the frantic cry of a mother, and then another's.

"'Immediately, there was a search for the infants and a manhunt. The mothers and the fathers were all too much distressed; lamentation and desperation had already driven them to madness. I, myself, their main chief and source of patience, couldn't think a thought straight, they all seemed too inconsistent. The senseless town scattered all about; there wasn't any organized procedure. Some looked in the ocean and some on the beach. Every hut was examined completely. They found the huge canoes on the beach and now the uncontrollable crowd realized that the abductees might be alive with the captors in the forest. I immediately commanded the men and the women to arm themselves with lances and bows and to roam the forest together. The mothers were soon possessed by a monstrous rage; they had to be detained. I ordered some men and women to find them some medicine. I suggested something like hope that lives hidden like a forgery or could work as an effective placebo, or something like induced oblivion that cures the pain of the spirit or quenches the thirst of the mind; but the doses were too little and the mothers rejected them all. Nonetheless, they were restrained and left behind as we all headed towards the dreadful forest. The fathers of the victims led the mob of ferocious Ciguayans. We heard foreign chants in the distance and we saw white smoke of a campfire in the starry sky. We hastened to the monstrous site and we found about sixteen repugnant creatures, (I refute to call them men), feasting on our small children. We heeded the racks with the intact fresh heads of the preys, and one of the fathers fainted and dropped to the ground; the other was speechless for a quick moment and suddenly a white hideous cry, rebellious even to the heaven, came out of the deepest part of his soul and he charged the guilty animals with all his strength, though it was vainly. The rugged savages, armed with sharp spears, seemed wont to the challenge. The man met his death in midair with a spear in his heart. A few of my men met the same misfortune.

"'The Caribs ran away from our fury as if fear were non-existent. They defiled our vengeance, and mocked our clamor for victory, and escaped to the beach, all except one that we managed to block. That wretched spirit ran into the forest and a few of my men pursued him. The rest of the villains approached their canoes with the throng of Ciguayans behind them. They pushed their canoes into the water and they navigated in the rough waves as they were sailing in gentle and even water. Meanwhile, the abandoned miserable rat, frightened like a coward, ran deep into the thick forest; he converted himself into a snake, a way of saying it, and they lost him.

"'I sent half the people of the village into the woods. The other half was to guard the beach. The strategy was to safeguard the beach and to shake and sweep the forest everywhere. There was no trace of the hidden man. They searched for him everywhere; but we knew he was still in our land. The stars disappeared from the sky; the moon was gone. They sought for him until the light of dawn appeared and they welcomed the first rays of light from the sun. They used the howling Indian siren for the first time when they saw the enemies; you and your innocent companions; they thought you were Caribs.

"'The mothers of the victim were informed of the tragic events. Madness consumed them like a demon would a weak soul. (I am old and cannot venture into the forest.) So I let the other eager half of my people undertake the task of their desire. I couldn't restrain the mad women no more; and on they went into the forest. I went after them and misfortune and old age stroked me when I fell onto my own pointed spear. When they were in the forest, they found the heads of their children in situ; their desolation was so deep that they recreated the horrible incident in their minds; then they fainted. The ephemeral inaction ended when the women were suddenly awakened by something unnatural; their spirits felt foreign; their human part frozen; they were possessed by the demons of hatred and vengeance; they ran into the forest with a despairing clamor, remorselessly, and the rest of the story is your own experience.'

"The old man stops his talk; a new affliction takes possession of his body; he coughs and breathes forcefully; he has a hidden wound in his chest. Now he must also worry about war and an augury. But all he sees in the man in front of him is the passive Taino—compassionate, gracious, and pious. This is Arixis's action before the old man: he gets out of the caney looking anxiously for fresh air and the presence of his god, Yucahu. He wishes the god to be a man like his own father. He takes an image of his goddess and he is reminded that the essence of his god lives in his imagination and the essence of his goddess wherever he feels his own temple. He opens his arms widely and drops his knees on the ground; he breathes the pure air and realizes the value of his goddess and the principle of his god. He says: 'Oh, Yucahu, forgive me, because now I realize that your grace can only be grabbed by whoever understands you. You are the air that I breathe, and I am so glad and lucky to breathe you that I will defend your presence with peace or war, and I promise to protect the space where this Taino lives, for without it, you and I are nothing. So Yucahu, you are the space, my constant thoughts, and my fruitful dreams. This awful experience contrived by nature only, your mother Yucahu, has shown me your immensity; you are therefore always growing in me.' He grabs tightly his

goddess in his hand and comes back to the caney.
He tells the chieftain this: 'My chief, this is the
beginning of a war; my father would never let our
misfortune go unnoticed. He is a pious man, and
fear, that necessary demon, personified in masks,
has been debated to be included in our celebrations.
He will wage war on you, for the sake of his god
and therefore for the sake of his people. I must
return at once and soften his heart with the truth.'

"The royal chief's eyes blink at the younger man's
intention. He takes off the feather-holding band,
without it he looks like a common powerless man.
His eyes roll and blink, and the chief struggles to
walk toward Arixis. He hugs the stranger and tells
him a secret. Soon he falls and faints in Arixis's
arms. The chief's garment is full of blood and now
Arixis's. Arixis holds the chieftain's band and
feather. The maids come back into the *caney* and
find a guilty scene. The princess cannot believe the
vision; a scream brings in the raggedy guards. The
behique rushes into the *caney* and Arixis is again
held as a prisoner.

First Vegan Carnival

IV

"The Holy Hill dresses inflamed with a timely sunset over the horizon. The multitude of Maguans awaits the chief's presence with dances and talks from communal leaders. A hush infiltrates as the chief enters the *batey*; the *behique* and some *nitainos* accompany him. Obviousness ranks the chief above all by the patented style of his attires, prohibited to commoners and nitainos. He is also distinguished by the way he is treated by the very sponsors of honor and dignity—the innocents and some of the elders. Even the fake nobles, with their hidden inconformity at life and nature, envy and admiration, desolation and happiness, render reverence to the mighty leader of their nation.

"The humble chief does not allow the announcer or even the insisting behique to introduce him to the crowd—the hush of the people has already done so. He tells them: 'Make god bless our children, our elders, and the core of this nation. Let us first thank the invisible creators for the visible things that they give and for the thoughts and feelings that are men and women. Let us ask them clearly and without mystery to keep for us what we share in common, the land and water of Magua—the gifts from a kind mother. We can give shelter to anyone that comes to our land, we would do that with honor, for it was freely given to us, but we cannot allow anyone to come and make the land and water uncommon; for it would mean the destruction of our tribe. Where would we find pride in that? Pride thrives in our living hearts, not in a dead body. We gave much thought to the conflict at hand. I will tell you what I have concluded after the exhausting conference with the elders, all the *nitainos*, and our brave and proud warriors; brave because they will go back and fight at your side and proud because they stand alive with us tonight.

"'War is bad. So we simply have to avoid its permanency, but a quick and strategic war we must have. Caution will lead our way and with patience the god of war will help us convene a mighty army. In two, three or four months we will invade North Macorix and help the Ciguayans regain their liberty. We will give them reason. That's our cause; that's our moral mission.'

"At the bonfire, the chief's wont to answer all types of questions from the nitainos, the elders, friends or rising commoners. A child of ten, now half an orphan, with watery eyes, and trembling knees, but very courageous, hurls a concern to the chief; it is cut in midair by his mother. The chief catches half his words and half the actions. He says: 'Let him talk, woman. Let him talk because the child seems to be concerned about something important.'

"The child says: 'My chief, they say that if a man of this tribe refuses to fight in this vital war, he is nothing but a coward. War, as you say, is bad and for that reason I now have no father. I don't want to be a coward, but my mother weeps and weeps and with tears she washes her face and keeps it clean. I also miss my father.' The chief and many are moved by his gentle words.

"The chief clears a knot in his throat and thinks before he answers him: 'My son, I will talk to you as I would talk to a man. It is a terrible lie they tell. There are no slaves in my tribe, no forceful duty to be performed and for the sake of nobody; a man is free to stay but the consequences might be dear. I heard the despairing comment that half the tribe may not join voluntarily, and yet I see a sea of heads rising. We will go to war to remedy the harm caused to your father and to prevent the plague of injustice from contaminating the rest of the village. Ask your mother, she does not weep because of the war or because of your farther, but because she is a warrior like your father. She will join us voluntarily

and you will stay in the village like the other
youngsters. In fine, your mother must leave you for
a while and she weeps because she will miss you.'

"The sentiment of war brings a common
camaraderie; the enemy is one and unknown his
figure. Half the Maguan men will venture into the
promised war and the other half will secure the
Maguan's valley. An elder woman expresses her
concern and once again Cibael is all ears. She says:
'My chief, the greatest good is to save a thriving
tribe; war can have an opposite effect, it is indeed a
detrimental evil. Even though my tribe has no trait
of cowardice, I assure you, revenge might leave us a
thousand widows. This war will make widows and
leave many women unmarried; it will deprive us of
our pride; if women are by nature to bear healthy
children, our men should not die in a war. What do
you think of the pride of bearing children?'

"'He says: 'It is indeed a very strong natural and
cultural pride; a kind that makes our women, too
passionately, fall in love with nature. If we don't
wage this war, the whole tribe, men, women, and
children, can face a horrible fate. Have faith, we
will not lose this war. I assure you, caution is at our
side. Every woman will be a mother and a
grandmother here; this war will not deprive our
women of this pride.' Then he jokes: 'If I come
back alive, I would marry a thousand of these
beautiful women; our hummingbirds tie themselves
with whomever, as long as the female type is native

to this valley. Believe me, by nature, there's good polygamy in the prairie.'

"The Taino tambours begin to beat slowly like the heart of the celebrations. The cacique relaxes for a while on his high seat as other speakers begin to teach from moral stories or express alternative opinions and detailed strategies about the foreseeable gory war. The short celebration, instead of instilling pride and quenching affliction, suggests departure, separation, and pain. They know that as soon as the sun comes out in the morning and offers them an arm of light, they will walk its entirety. Somehow, by a chance of nature, pessimism and anticipated nostalgia crawl on the ground of the Holy Hill. The great chief notices the young, slender Taino men, in the golden mean of life, preparing for the war; all seem unquiet of soul. Some young mothers hide their tears as they sense a separation from husbands or sons, and older women protest the quick departure and question the urgency; although the warriors will not face an enemy in months but construct an alliance first. The royal chief realizes the commotion and runs quickly toward the behique; he asks him for the relief and the behique signals at some people: the musicians come out onto the stage.

"First, the quick metrical sound of the *güira* introduces a parade of boys and girls; they're all singers in the chorus. Their song is patriotic; they allude to the town and their most basic childish hope: to run freely, to climb fruitful trees, and to

72

swim in the stream. There's no religion intertwined in the message and nostalgia is not a theme. The behique feels satisfied with the performance; the people are all drawn in. The sound of maracas changes the mood and a group of young people brings another cultural bonanza to the bonfire.

"A file of noble princesses dances out of the near forest onto the light created by the fire. They circle the fire and the men fix their eyes in the appeasement of affliction and uncertainty. The beautiful women slant their steps towards their husbands, already dressed as warriors; they step away from them, and continue the dance in file. As they step away from them, the women throw kisses at the men with their hands and flirtatious looks that incite alliance.

"The thud of the tambours and the quick chun-chun of the *güiras* spur a male-female friendly rivalry. Within the crowd a person screams the word 'Tainos', then another similar scream with the word 'women' and another with the word 'men' follow until the whole crowd is parted in two factions. Women keep their dances and now the brave men come out of the crowd; they form pairs with the women, they confront them and compete to show which gender is the strongest, and at the end the women claim to win the dancing battle.

"They all scream the word 'women' in unison, but the men in the happy crowd jeer at all the women in the game. But in turn, the women in the crowd begin the sound of war, a siren of crisis. Solidarity comes with the sound of the word 'Taino' and its echoes emanating from the throats of children, men, and women. The players embrace their loved ones; then they shake with fear at the thudding sound of the Taino tambours. Now the devils, representing the evils within a person, enter the sacred stage of fire. These men wear masks made with the vivid expression of horrified monkeys; their souls sucked in by the mere essence of suffering; they intentionally frighten the children in the crowd. Then they come after the male players and devour them all, one by one, until only the princesses remain. The screams of horror terrify them all and they run madly around the bonfire until the cacique, with his might truncheon, stands tall on the spotlight; he also holds a torch of purity. The princesses run quickly towards the protector of the good people, and the cacique swings his torch and feints at the devils with his baton, and one by one the devils faint and drop to the holy ground. The music stops and a hush falls from heaven suddenly.

"The cacique addresses the crowd: 'Taino people, I created sweet liquor from the bitter part of yucca and maize; it is a gift for this celebration. We might call this a good night now.' The crowd cheers. Jars of the liquor seem to spring from the ground. The demons or the devils are deposed of their horrible masks and they become happy men as they reunite with their friends and families. They now drink and dance to the rhythm of the tambours, the maracas and the güiras. The compass of the lively music releases them from a person's animal instinct. The whole crowd is once again emerged in the celebration. All themes are lost for a while; they talk just to talk; they dance just to dance; they sing just to sing.

"The liquor, the conversation, the dances and the songs are passions that nobody can resist for too long, but one more than the other. Yet, the children have already gone to bed with their mothers. The tambours sound is put off by exhaustion, and the night, heavy with liquor, sits on the eyelid of every standing man. Thus, the first Vegan carnival is completed.

March to Maguana

V

"Bajacu's presence, before the first ray of light from the sun, still under the rays of the crescent moon, drives Cibael out of his hammock. He lights a few burning sticks of wood for the mild chilling air of the uncertain war and the beautiful clarity that allows him to detect the invaluable existences of his main wife and his baby son. This captivates the royal chief's heart and instantly the chief finds himself next to his son, who is calmly sleeping on his hammock. Cibael holds the baby on his arms and his son's breathing soul makes him smiles.

"Cibael is an experienced man, but Yucahu has dropped the fountain of youth on him and all his kindness; his strength and look represent the image of a thirty-year-old man. (Lying abounds in stories, but Cibael is the real deal). His main wife, (there wasn't a more beautiful woman among the ancients), wakes up happily for she has felt the king amusing her youngest son in her dream.

"Arixis, her beloved son, paints his vivid image in her mind by divine power. 'He's alive,' she says and the smooth whisper gives Cibael a pleasant hope. 'And he is very very happy. A mother's instinctive pain got to the deepest part of my soul,' she tells the joyful man with confidence.

"Cibael replies: 'Woman, I am holding him in my arms; I feel his heart beating; he's very much alive, and he is happy indeed for he smiles as I speak.'

"Confusion steps at side: 'No, I feel his blood flowing and I am not even touching him; it's not your last I am talking about, but your first, Arixis,' the queen emphasizes.

"Cibael approaches her and embraces her passionately, and still holding the baby on his arms, he says: 'Pain as you know it is not a good thing. You cannot misinterpret it as an animate hope. When you get these happy moments by feeling, do not confound them with sufferings. If this occurs, hope in you is dead, or maybe there wasn't any to begin with. He is alive because he's alive, and nobody has given us the proof that he is dead. We could be denying heaven and earth, but the fact that we are going to war is a testament of our love, not of out suffering. So inspirit your mind, woman! Enliven it to the fullest! Enliven it because the mere wind does blow away the ash of the fire, but it does not blow away that of the spirit. So that there isn't any ash, do not light sticks of wood or any inflammable things in your head. Suffering for a common supposed event is not a sure thing. Aren't we noble? We deal with the truth, woman. Cheer up woman! Cheer up!! Your suffering was an ephemeral thing!' She foreknows his departure to the war, and she embraces him and gives him a kiss; the hope is very much alive.

"Cibael brings the prince back to its comfortable hammock. The magic of love makes the demigod and his queen appear under the silver moonlight. The Taino king brings his mate on his arms. Behind the *caney*, the chief has planted a garden of beautiful flowers, and there's also a rectangular patch of grass, facing the seeming reachable crescent moon; that moon has seen fire there. He takes his most precious flower and places her on the bed of grass; his intention is to defoliate her gently. She is an *Esperanza* that draws him to kiss her and breathe her and to feel her entirely, sweet from lips to toes; she likes the heat of the day and the nocturnal passion. Her passion rises and it is most felt with the heat of the dry weather, and it drops under the wet weather. They feel as if they have been stripped of their bodies and their mere souls collide once and twice and thrice and more. The stamen enters the pistil and fertilizes the stigma with an ardent desire. Blossoming is not instantaneous, but the action seems to be very rejuvenating. The queen looks brighter under the fading moon and the royal chief possesses a new hope. The birds of the valley begin to chirp and with them the men and women of the village awake.

"Back in the royal hut, the chief prepares for his journey. He takes his best bow and chooses the best arrows and spears. The chief is an artist and the best athlete of the lance and the arrow; likewise he is the best swimmer, fisherman, farmer and philosopher of his land. He is armed for all adversities.

"In the meantime, the eager warriors, accompanied by all their families, wait for the chief in the *batey*. A chief-general has them in files, facing the *caney*. They begin to sing a war song that incites patriotism. The royal chief comes out of the threshold of the *caney*, and he encounters all the highest ranking stakeholders or household heads at his door; the behique makes his way to the right side of the royal chief. The sea of warriors and all the *nitainos* are all prepared for the expected belligerence.

"The Maguan cacique addresses his people once again: 'Maguans, today's journey is the most difficult challenge that our nation has faced. It is indeed the most consequential and odd. We look for unity and yet we part from our families and from our village. Now remember my saying, the spirit of our nation is alive and its heart beats with passion.

We hold the greatest responsibility in our hands, but with each step and each decision our duty increases its magnitude; the weight of our village is heavy, but we will also defend our greater Magua, and our alliance seeks to protect the spirit of Kiskeya. So, let us create an alliance of kinship among Maguans first. When one of us dies, the spirit of our nation weakens; but the suffering caused by our losses is an indication that our divine spirit is strong, for we are yet together; yet we prefer the gain of a soul in a body and a happy smile in an infant as better indicators of our strength; that's why we go to war now. We will protect Magua with our hearts and souls first.'

"The great commander delegates half his nation to the north, excluding the children, the elders and pregnant women; the other half will accompany him to the south. The north delegation spreads through the valley, east and west. They all carry their goddess with them; she will remind them of their origin and their humanity. They also carry caution in their heads, especially those that will roam the valley of death.

"In days a group of Maguan arrives at Guárico, agitated and worried, with a pleading message of unity. The main cacique is in a foreign mission, but they are received with love and affection. They deliver the urgent message. But urgency is not a thing with priority in this land. The sense of war is lost and all the Maguans feel the calmness of the people. Even caution seems to rest on a hammock, compelled by the feeling of peace. But in the valley of death, caution brings bitter moments. In days the Maguans have not slept or sung or breathed in and out the pure air of the valley with peace of mind. In two days the demons must have slept in their thoughts only; they were very inactive. Soon, misfortune strikes again. The missing Cariban scoundrel appears, walking on the forest. He sees a single Taino admiring the birds on a tree. He thinks the careless man is a Ciguayan. Furtively, he approaches the warrior and seizes him from behind; he maneuvers his stony knife and coldly slits his throat. Another Maguan catches a glimpse of the evil action and sounds the siren of danger. The Cariban man runs away to find himself surrounded by a throng of angry Vegans. The siren is unending; it quickly travels the entire forest. All the Maguans come to the danger; the daring act of a cannibal Caribs. The Cariban man tries to run away, but finds Vegans everywhere. Suddenly, an arrow pierces his throat and a hundred more his whole body. The Maguans look everywhere for more enemies, but there aren't any Caribs in that forest. Nonetheless, the news becomes a gossip and travels quickly across the forest. It says that the situation is well controlled, but that Caribs are spread in the Maguan valley. Now, they only wait at the side of caution and fear consumes their morale and their hearts make them feel like cowards; even the gentle flight of the hummingbirds seems a menace. They obey Cibael's command. They keep their distance from the border of Macorix and soon realize that the valley is friendly. The days go by in peace and the *nitainos* build their huts and live their lives with caution; and they know that one day the warring smoke from a bonfire will rise and they will invade North Macorix from within; that is their destiny.

"Meanwhile, Cibael marches south toward Maguana with the most fervent and rugged warriors of Magua. Their confidence makes them dauntless of heart and they would prefer to live fighting for the sake of their nation, fearless of any barricades. Their hearts beat joyfully even though they know that their fate is uncertain. So, they proudly carry spears, bows, and arrows on both shoulders and in both hands; these remind them of danger. Though, they sing and sing, and they dance and dance once a day with the approval of their captain, their general, their royal chief. Then, some throw and hang their hammocks between coconut trees or mango trees, while others lay their heads on the grass and rest peacefully. The royal chief always takes his time to light a cigar or smoke from a pipe for relaxation. His tobacco is pure, cultivated in his fertile land with water and sun and nothing else. So, Cibael leans on a tree smoking the leaves of pleasure that came from his valley. Yucahu is on his mind.

"The behique and two other noble chiefs critique their leader from the distance. The behique comments on his sane habit: 'The habit extends from his ancestors. The cultivation of his plants exceeds theirs in excellence. He brags about his knowledge of tilting the plants so that they feed life from the generous sun. His ancestors worshipped that bright star and the custom seems to remain alive in him, for in the morning he has been seen lifting his hands to the heavens and thanking the deity for the excellent shape of the leaves. He claims the plant transmits calmness and there lies the reason for smoking it. If every man possesses a bit of craziness, there in the field one would notice his share. He tilts, waters, and kisses every single one of his plants. Inadvertently, I once stepped into his garden to deliver a message; I touched his foliage leaves, and he came madly toward me, grabbed my neck and threatened to kill me. He said that my folly could have gotten him killed by putting my dirty hands on the purity of his calmness. He beseeched me never to enter his garden again or else it would be the decline of the purity of his art and that of tranquility.'

"And one of the chiefs adds: 'It is such a calamity that partaking of perfection the man seeks refuge under a decaying shelter. I can only imagine the day when corrupted men own the land of Magua, and division of the chief's territory—under a thousand greedy heads—creates the evil of slavery. Cacibajagua was pure and divine until a chief conquered the people's hearts and he became the first cacique. There are five now in Kiskeya. Cibael lives in the blossoming of Magua, but the man believes in the present and denies the future for he thinks it a burden; that is his suffering. But like every existing thing, Magua will decay and will evolve and it will die. He fights to remain in power and to protect it. The man evolves for being a living thing; the man is a demigod when seen individually and a god collectively. Cibael saw in you and me demons; for the gossip goes that you as I asked him for private pieces of land, and truly he denied our requests; Magua is only the noble man's land. He told me: <Will I be able to give everyone an equal share, or only an unequal share to the *nitainos*? If the latter stands, imagine the slavery it will create on those that possess no land. You will have to kill a man a day or they will live one on top of the others as if they were birds on a tree, or as if they were boars in sties, competing for the given food; and if they are men, the lamenting cries of women will never cease; and blood will flow on roads and on hidden places; men will always strive for survival, not to obtain perfection. They say that Magua belongs to me, and I agree for I belong to Maguans.>. That's the man you see inclining on that tree; a man unequal to men, a hater of wars, and yet a pure warrior. So, there's no surprise that a sycophant—gifted with oratory and imitation—be expelled from his garden in the hour of the chief's quiescence." So, the chief ends his comments and as if by natural consent, the participants disperse and find their niche of rest. The Royal chief is now the only one awakened.

"The sun, the moon, and the earth redden together the sky, and the trees of the Maguan forest move violently as Cibael's warriors sleep away their fatigue. The royal chief inspects the firmament and the syzygy smoothly fades; the moon, the sun, and the earth are not forgotten in his thoughts, and the starry night pacifies the tides in the distant ocean. The Cacique walks about the forest, east and west, north and south, a radius of safety, and his heart confesses to his blood his trust in nature. The sticks of wood fly on to his hands as if by the magic of his god, who is always at his side, and he carries them to an empty space among the green lungs of the earth; and then the royal chief artfully builds the frame of a bonfire. Casks of liquor unpack magically from bundles of cotton, and cassava and hunted birds are seasoned by the Cacique and placed on the barbecue's frame. The rest of his company still rests.

"Guatauba, sent by the mere god of nature, pokes the warriors as if with a tingling sword; they wake happily one by one, rested, yawning and stretching their arms fully. A hiding moon accompanies the distant stars in the cosmos, and the Tainos, naturally, yield to the rhythm of the smooth night of the Maguan forest. The Taino tambours begin to beat slowly and a group of warriors in a file circle the yet lit bonfire. The royal chief strikes the stones and the sparks become a flame and the wood a fire. On the sides of the bonfire, the roasting birds begin to diffuse the savory smell from the barbecue. Soon, all souls are awakened and the nightly festivity is in full blossom. Some drink wildly; others eat temperately, and some dance to the rhythm of the tambours and the *güiras*; and some smoke uncorrupted tobacco from pipes and stuffed rolled-up leaves. Cibael unnoticeably absents himself from the crowd and finds a comfy bed of leaves under a huge tree; there he rests until the coming morning.

"The brightest white star that the Maguans see rises up from the east. Cibael—seeming like the bravest of warriors—stands between two trees, facing east and looking at the goddess's wonder. Then, the chief's siren commands the warriors to scatter strategically in the forest, and quickly they're all positioned and ready to continue their journey as the sun hits the horizon. They walk tirelessly singing a belligerent song when suddenly the royal chief suspends their chant in midair, and human voices, excited and jovial, chant the hymn that proclaims the creation of a new village and his cacique. Still in Maguan territory, steps away from the border, all the brave men and women crouch under bushes and lie on the ground at the possible existence of danger; they wait actively for the command of their leader—the wisest men on earth to them. Cibael camouflages among the trees and furtively approaches and analyzes the site, hiding among friendly bushes. He determines that these people are Tainos from Maguana; he recognizes their distinctive accent. His instinctive fear leaves his noble heart; but precaution still touches his adept mind; he has not been informed of this new flow of people settling so close to his border.

"He sends two agile Maguans to enter the new settlement. Dozens of new huts are scattered on small hills. Men and women raise their arms to greet them from the distance as they now pass by their huts on the Maguanan roads; all the roads lead to the *batey*. They experience the flavor of the Maguanan culture as they walk. They modify their dialect, and to reduce their Maguan accent, they try their best classic Taino. Here's the painting from their eyes. A young man still sleeps on his hammock, hanging between two palm trees. An old man leans on a tree, watching and listening to the pleading a young man makes to his beloved. His proposed verses are these:

"'Every morning I leave my house my heart's nostalgic beats grow crazily. The pain I feel when I part from your side is a mere disease of the soul; my cure is the proximity to my woman's kissing lips. She tames my worried heart with the thoughts of kissing and hugging her every night; but a short distance is a cruel spear stabbed in my heart; so I'd rather live in the border of her bones.

"'You are my woman; your hug is a shield that protects me from nostalgia and your warmth is a magnet that attracts me to your side. So woman, let a man hug you and kiss you once more; for a sweet kiss and a warm hug make a man return to his woman like the waves of the ocean that always return to the shore.'

"The Maguans spies march freely and worriless on the roads of the new village. The children smile as they play their favorite ball game that they call *batú*.

Someday glory will accompany them as they play in the *batey*. So the spies mingle with the children and teach them some skilled techniques of their own. The game goes on with imitations as the spies extract themselves out of the flow of the game. Up ahead, some boys and girls tattoo their bodies as the spies approach them and show them new ideas for the noble drawings. Not far away, an ancient man smoke some tobacco on a rotten pipe and the Maguans show him how to put the dry leaves on a perfect roll; so much in such a little time will the Maguanans learn from the Cibaons.

"The proud Tainos reach an open meeting and notice the future chief in the *batey*. The Nitaino chief had been assigned by the royal chief of Maguana to his new post. Shouts and joy, from the loyal faction and the nitainos, completely filled with sympathy and admiration help the Vegans be overlooked and their diminutive difference fades as they are now Maguanans. Soon, the Vegans and the true supporters lift the cacique up in the air. He flies freely with open arms over the excited crowd and the ardent devotees. Several times he rounds the batey until the cheering fades naturally and he lands on the stage of the batey to quickly make a proclamation. He commands (in a nutshell) the day to erupt with joy of celebration. Willing collaboration injects into the opponents' blood, (those you crave for the chief's position), and envy diminishes with the arrival of jars of liquor, food, dances, and the prepared carnival. Beautiful women dance with the cacique and the sycophants, too. The exclamations of unceasing joyful voices linger in the air. Now, one of the Vegans catches an opportunity to advance his mission. The clever and deceitful Vegan conquests all eyes and throws their sights on him. Their attraction is a treacherous dance that allows the Maguan to be like the sun; all the bodies rotate about him. His contagious moves spread and everywhere the Maguan sees imitators. "Now, the lonely star lost in the universe is approached by the other Vegan. He squeezes himself among the people and the guardians of the chief. The chief, as if by magic, is drawn to the edge of the forest and the Vegan gives him a blow to the neck. Soon, the sun loses its illustrious present as the other stars begin to emerge in the universe, and the Maguan becomes himself a shadow. He goes into the forest and meets with his comrade and the fainted chief. They place the chief on their shoulders and divide the weight in two; they fly with the raised cacique among the trees of the forest.

"The chief, unconscious by the stroke, is taken to the feet of a king. Yet, his absence in the *batey* goes unnoticed. The fuss and festivities unceasingly hold his throne. The commoners in any celebration ascend one step above the sycophants in nature. Men and women celebrate, and the sycophants painfully enjoy, in oblivion, for their commonality surfaces above their inferiority complex. Their chief is temporarily forgotten; or truly, he's not needed.

"Meanwhile, Cibael sprays the new chief's face with clean water; he strikes his cheeks gently. The set of slight strikes is the antidote to the chief's heavy slumber. He wakes up seeing everything in pieces and the strange faces clack into a full image. The chief gets up as if in a panic and like a rat, by instinct, tries to find an escape to security—all in vain. He is circulated by the shield of Maguans.

"He realizes the king's convoy is impenetrable. He calms down, but still boldly, for he is a true warrior, says: 'Who are you? Why do you use injustice as your weapon? Do you even realize the danger you put yourself in?'

"Cibael answers him: 'No danger from you we guess. Do you realize the danger that you are in?'

"'Why have you kidnapped me? Where do you come from? Maguana will not receive you well and there's nothing you will take from her, for she is stronger than a rock, and more resilient than time.'

"Then Cibael: 'You sound like a desperate patriot. But if humbleness keeps residing away from your heart, your land will survive the test of time for a while. But I have seen with my own eyes the decaying effects of thoughts and nobility, and I have discovered that even some ideas seem to have half-lives. We did the injustice as you call it because we don't know who you people are. Look at the ground I stand on. Don't you smell the essence of Magua? Now I realize that you could be friends, steps away from our borders. To us, Magua is the most beautiful thing that the goddess has created. In a brink of an eye, on her edge, Magua has a new village; I thought I was well-informed of Maguana's growth. I leave the words to you.'

"The chief replies to the man: 'Maguana is the most beautiful thing that the goddess has created. Yet, it seems that intruders have stepped into her private room and sequestered one of her child for unknown intention. I ask again, besides being Maguans, who are you? What do you want from me?'

"Cibael's behique approaches the chief and says: 'Relax, my brother, put down your invisible spear and let your soul breathe out your anger and your fear. We are Maguans and the master chief of Magua stands as an equal at your side; Cibael's a friend and a brother of Maguana. Have you knowledge of our sufferings, you would have considered your injustice as our precaution. Surely, it seems that we owe you an apology, but listen to our misfortune in brief.' The behique recounts briefly the bitter moments.

"Now, the chief prostrates himself in front of Cibael. The landowner's fame touches the lips of the Tainos in every village. After all, Cibael is one of the five great masters of Kiskeya—the most sublime land for these Tainos. Cibael is silent as he rejects the infamous custom—men kneeling in front of another as if the one standing were a god. He feels a parade of roughly formed icicles, as hard as rocks, running through his veins, and then destroying every fiber of his body. He wishes to say this: 'Stand up and speak to me as an equal. Here in Magua we are brothers; here equality is real.' But he knows well that the chief will reject his preposition for it would be an ill-constructed lie. Instead, Cibael leaves the task to his behique.

"The behique tells the chief: 'Stand up, feel yourself as an equal and speak like one.' The chief realizes that Cibael approves the command with honesty and an ephemeral ignorance; he feels his docility to the idea and the chief rises up, now fearlessly.

"He tries to praise the royal chief: 'Great chief, you are one of the fairest persons in all the earth. The gossip tells that your intelligence is hidden in mere altruism. Maguana's master is my father, and this makes you my uncle. Words from your lips have been repeated in my house since I was a child. Our blood is red and has the same density. Your thoughts and your beliefs are part of our culture. So, please, tell your behique not to hurt me with insults; his mockery of equality can cause a deep wound; it makes me want to ask for mercy. Isn't Magua your land? Who do the people ask permission in your village? Don't you live in a caney with your goddess? Why does the great Cibael have a dozen guards dedicated solely to his security? I tell you the reason; Cibael is an angel in the people's eyes. He is a small sun that shines as he speaks. He is a god who molded the mere shape of Magua. His thinking is the present and the partial future. His

actions are the closest things to justice; but
inequality has a crown of its own in Magua. It
seems that Cibael denies the power of the sun; but
the sun's splendor has already left a shadow in
Maguana. Maguana is the center of Kiskeya; his
royal chief is its sun; and he is aware of it.
Shouldn't the master of Magua be aware of his
dominion?'

"The chief's intended praise creates a reaction. The
behique replies: 'You speak like a true bold Nitaino.
It marvels me to hear how you extract an insult out
of an act of kindness. No doubt you must have a
noble heart. Favoritism exists in Magua, but
benevolence controls it. Inequality is apparent as
you have discerned it, but sweet words adorn it as
pleasure and it feels better. I didn't hurl an insult at
you; you caught one out of thin air and hurled it at
our noble chief, the man you now call your ignorant
uncle. He told you about the test of time, and you
did not mind him or you did not understand him.
Man is not an image of the God, but a part of it. Our
chief is well aware of the man's desire to be like the
God; he has to make decisions that hurt him deeply.
The moral man is an idea that evolves, and when
corrupted, goes astray from perfection.'

"The royal chief tells them: 'Enough, come here
son, and hug a friend, an uncle, a father.'
Confidence gives the chief a friendly push and he
hugs his uncle. The chief smiles and the warriors
approach him friendly; the amicable air spreads in a

circle and all sit on the ground to learn from the chief about his people.

"The chief briefly recounts the state of Maguana: 'Maguana is a powerful land. There is a Yucayeque, a Taino village, every certain distance. Twin huts, at midpoint between two villages, house two families of warriors for six patriotic months. Their duty is to carry messages from villages to villages and to keep our royal chief well-informed. In the South Sea, Maguanan canoes are present day and night. The royal chief is glorified truly and falsely. But the details of Maguana's growth can be recount in a more comfortable place. Be my guests, I implore you. Come and join the festivities in the batey.' They all walk toward the village.

Land and Soul

The Great Jaragua

VI

"As Cibael, his warriors, and the new cacique enter the small village, a gossip spreads from mouth to mouth and from hut to hut. The great royal chief of Cibao has invaded Maguana. As Cibael enters the batey, some of the villagers are astonished by the demigod's presence. They prostrate themselves in reverence to the man. Cibael is astonished at the gesture and he takes it as it comes. The music and dances come to a stop and the new chief introduces the great Cacique of Magua. The celebration continues until the stars shine in the sky and only the stronger souls stay awake by the bonfire. Another gossip spreads to overwrite the first one; Cibael is paying a friendly visit to Maguana.

"Now, the new chief, sitting on his *dujo*—the decorated seat of the nitainos—smokes some tobacco, a gift from Cibael, and prepares to deliver his promise. He claims that the stories of Maguana and Jaragua are fraternal twins. So, he tells them:

"'The Great Yagua, the master of Jaragua, and his tribe are thrown and scattered on the land by the god of destiny. His burden is a dagger in the throat of a lost *cinzontle*; each family of the tribe wants its independence, but all the songs are not sung with the same tone. (Magua began as one and is becoming many, but Jaragua began as many and it is becoming one.)

"'Each and every painful cry of life or complaint of the soul is attributed to the innocent master of the land. Mild envy, like dirty smoke, or the dark fog of the night, pollutes the clear air of Jaragua. People clash on the roads and many families are raided by the indigenous clans of Jaragua. The Great Yagua, the protector of Casibajaguans, now bombarded with spears and arrows, envy and rivalry from the indigenous clans and from within his own kin, gathers his own immediate kinfolks and takes them to the heart of Jaragua. There he founds Yaguana; he orders his own house, and peace begins to reign within his small village.

"'Now, the lost *cinzontles* fly from trees to trees in the unamicable land of Jaragua; they begin to hear harmonious songs in Yaguana; songs inspired by Zuimaco and the creator of shrewdness and compassion. They fly to Yaguana, begging the master of that land to cage them and guide them forever. And since diversity, when it works toward one goal, is a blessing upon a people, in days, Yaguana grows from its adolescence to adulthood; in months, it becomes the biggest *yucayeque* of Kiskeya. It feels like the lost cinzontles have found their way north.

"'Outside of Yaguana, Jaragua has pocket villages of Casibajaguans; yet they outnumber the indigenous clans everywhere. No mountain is safe, no cave is secure, and no village is a haven. The clans clash on the roads; fishermen contend on the abundant sea, and the growers are threatened with drought of words in the ample land. But, the Tainos keep consuming the soul of the indigenous culture little by little; that's their biggest dispute.

"'Meanwhile, Yaguana is like a magnet for all the Casibajaguans of Jaragua; their chief is the mere core. Yucahu appears to the Great Yagua while he smokes a roll of pure tobacco under a Jaraguan tree. He contrives to bring the chiefs and their followers to an *areito* in Yaguana. He invokes the best poets and poetesses, the best singers and the musicians, the best orators and the politicians, the best healers and the astronomers, the best batú players and canoe athletes, and the best artists and the artisans. Some will prostrate as reverence to his presence at the beginning of the areito; all will prostrate at the end of the areito.

"'Now, the royal chief of Yaguana, days after his vision, having thought of all the necessary events, invokes his principal wife—his main ally—who will order and orchestrate the great carnival. With the task at hand, she prays to Guatauba for help. Soon, the god consents, and the rumor spreads to every corner of Jaragua. The mere god, disguised as a loyal Nitaino, visits every lord of the land of Jaragua, and they feel attracted by the importance of the gesture; they are asked to contribute to the massive festival. Meanwhile, a gossip also walks on the road of Jaragua; it goes from door to door, inviting the commoners—the best of their trades will be ascended to the rank of the nobles.

"'So, the great day comes. Everyone gathers for the festivities contrived by the Great Yagua, and designed by his most beloved wife. Taino drums beat in unison and the sound suspends itself at the same distance of time. The sound of the güiras emerges with the decrescendo of the tambours. The chun-chun repeats at a harmonious rate, and then the tambours reemerge and mix in the air; the *batey* is alive.

"'Suddenly, a hush falls on the batey. Only the sound of steps of female dancers emanates from the quietude; a file comes from the east and another from the west. And then the music accompanies the dancers onward to the bonfire. They circle the fire once and twice. They gather together in a circle, and the royal chief appears in the middle as if by magic; the music dies and a gasp is heard among the crowd. The loyalists all prostrate at his presence and a sense of disrespect overcomes the guests for not doing the same. The chief feels victorious as he waves his hands, greeting the crowd and again the music appears and the static dancers revive and the chief, within magical smoke, disappears. So the first dance of the show ends and the tambours begin to beat once again.

"'Then a singer comes out of the crowd and meets the dancers. Her words are these: <Kiskeya, created by the goddess of nature, bless your son, the great chief of this land. Give him the vision to reap good fruits for the people. Oh, Zuimaco, my heart, my blood, my moon, and my air, never consume my chief and let him live as your son, a god, on this earth. And you, Yucahu, who create thoughts, (invisible must your presence be!), make us realize that we are part of you as much as we are part of your divine mother.> Then she sings.

"'Then, a parade of singers and musicians, poets and poetesses, politicians and artisans crosses the center stage to portray the mere soul of the Taino people. At a strategic point, the chief's wife—a poetess, a story-teller, a politician, an astronomer, a lover of the Taino people—takes the stand. As the designer of the contrivance, she paves a smooth road for the entrance of the royal chief; her words are these: <My people, let Yucahu bless you with humanity. Zuimaco is with us as we speak. Some of us deny her power, but have you ever thought that we think; and if we think, and Yucahu is us, why

can't you imagine the things that are in our power?
Now, every Taino loves Yucahu, because they
know that he is their life. If you have taken notes,
you've known that every song and every complaint
mentioned the spirit of the god. You want to be
safe, and Yucahu is your life. The biggest threats in
your life are the vulnerable aboriginals; some of
whom have Taino blood running through their veins
already. So let us ask, who are the aboriginals and
why do we fight them?

"'<Well, they are the rebels of the land that we
inhabit, and they wouldn't change their land for
anything. They are very conservative and they're
not at all submissive. War to them is peace, and
peace is death, not change. Reason kills them one
by one. They claim that they were the first ones
here, and everywhere they see strangers and new
things. And yet their deepest pain comes from a
mortal wound to their progeny; they die in a
peaceful war. Their daughters and their sons play
enthusiastically Taino games. They fall in love
under the Taino sky. Their god is Yucahu and
Atabey is their goddess. Their joy has been taken
from their hearts and they have been left with
loneliness. The aborigines will never be slaves to
our culture; they will fight to death because
Kiskeyan people are brave by nature. So, be alert
and learn from them because some day we could be
in their own predicament.

"'<Who are the aboriginals? Humans! They are not merciful when their hearts have been bittered by reason of injustice. Do not let them deceive you once more. Let me remind you of Teteyoa's story. The Siboney's princess comes to me crushed by the weight of injustice, or so goes her claim. She manages to pass through a breach among the crowd, and nose-dives herself to my feet; her laments and tears can commove even the deities in the heavens. The guards point their spears at her head, but only tears flow from her eyes and kisses caress my feet. I see a mass of sorrow in front of me. I order the guards to relent, and instead of being cautious, they help the woman to stand in front of me. There, she stands, as beautiful as any imagined princess, undistinguishable her smile, her grace undeniable. Yet, abundant tears flow out of her eyes; there's a soul to be pitied inside her. Suddenly, a guard recognizes her shape, her beauty, and her rank. He comes towards me as if to warn me of a fire. He says: 'Mistress! Mistress! The woman that stands at your side is one of your biggest enemies. She's the Siboney's chief's daughter.' My pity vanishes in an instance. A gasp comes out of my mouth and pity again reappears. Pitiable Teteyoa is dragged away from me. Her mind is still silent as she looks behind at me with watery and hopeless eyes. But then, the goddess gives her courage and she defies the strength of men. She escapes their arms and plunges herself into my arms and embraces me now asking for compassion. The guards grab her by the arms and hair. Danger I see none, but fear possesses every nerve of my body and reasoning quenches it

with a second look at the poor girl. I order my guards to release her once again.

"'<'I am such a girl,' she says. 'But allow me to seek refuge and alliance under a Taino shelter. Listen to my pleadings at least.' Then, confusion invades your Queen's mind. (The Great Yagua, the purest of men, had commanded the eldest and the youngest of his court to run away from inconsistency.) I try to run away from Teteyoa and her pleadings drag me back to the pitiable vision. (The Great Yagua, the noblest of spirits, had told us of the evil of compassion in time of war. He also told us that our compassion is a lance often aimed and hurled at our heart by our enemy.) But I reason now that Teteyoa is a sack of sorrow and palming her back could bring calmness to my soul. She takes refuge under my arms. I bid her speak her mind, but tears and nerves block and tighten her throat and sobs over sobs squeeze out of it.

"'<'Take this poor soul to my private hut and tend to her needs. I will come and console her when time gives me leave.' I see the defenseless soul sigh out loudly; I am also relieved by the burden of compassion. The princess has now won my heart, and yet I do not know the source of her pains. (I had defiled my husband's command; he had told us that women would do anything to save their tribe. Siboney women would turn the world upside down if need be.)

"'<Later that same day, I meet with Teteyoa in my humble private hut. The princess now smiles and grace gives her a noble look. I am astonished at her beauty. But once she sees me, sadness descends on her body and she prostrates at my feet as if I were a goddess. 'Stop mourning woman, stand up, look into my eyes and tell me the source of your afflictions,' I say.

"'<She stands up and answers me with nobility: 'My tribe is dying.' The Great Yagua's warning comes out poking me in my ears. 'My parents accuse me of treason and their words always conjure a verdict. If treason is saving one's nation, I am as guilty as the act itself.'

"'<'What have you done to deserve such a verdict?'

"'<'I have fallen in love with a common Taino man and his culture. I have sat many times in your areito to hear your voice and that of your husband. Though you may not know my actions, I am also your biggest ally. Maybe, my mistress, you, who still possess noble blood, could understand me clearly.'

"'<'Elaborate on your saving deeds from beginning to end. I have patient ears.'

"'<'Yucahu, my god, brought him into my village as your tribe was brought into Jaragua. We were

104

innocent children with no gods or goddesses. Our parents prohibited us from mingling with classic Taino children. We always hid among the bushes as they played Gods and Goddesses. They imitated everything that the adults did in the areito. And once, Yucahu descended from the heaven and ordered us to defy our parents, and we crossed the rivulet to play with the Taino children. Our agonizing tribe breathed pure air and fed itself a healthy meal. We discovered Yucahu, the glue of the Taino people.

"'<'Then, we injected the idea of Yucahu in our games; and the years flew quickly into our future. We, the sickly children of this world, absorbed the substance of him, who gives hope to the dying, and hope became the blood of our game, and the game's heart started to beat, unceasing like the splashes of the brine, clashing on pebbles, stones, and rocks. The memories of time grew stronger and heavier, and father's denial drew blood into a dying culture.

"'<'As the young begin to live, the old begin to die. The Taino children spread like bad weeds in a fertile land; their songs influenced our singing; their music became our music, and like a contagious disease their language overtook our language; nonetheless, Yucahu's presence gladdened the youth and infuriated the elders. O rage, how slowly and painlessly your lunacy can kill a tribe! The elderly declared war on everything marked 'Taino'. A heavy blame, like a piece of heaven, fell on Yananini, my secret and beloved man. They put a bounty on his head; only to realize that it was easy to kill a man but not a good idea; the Taino man lives over adversity and the Siboney man dies by an idea. O, how furious were the elderly when an epidemic of impregnated Siboney's girls suddenly appeared! The Tainos were to blame.

"'<'A Taino hut emerged by the lake, its belly swollen with a litter, and its spirit a mere howler; impregnated with hopes, and joys; keeper of an invisible god, a true guardian, and the image of the goddess of plenty. The cry of life howled in the wind with the passion of a beast, and then it burst a hundred huts in days.

"'<'In days our homes were full of hopes and joys, and a visible god. Oh, how insane was the old man going! He denied fruition and joys, but he still saw our tribe dying. In a gathering he exclaimed: 'Has corruption crippled your senses? A woman sees unseen images; a man hears whispers in the wind; a child talks to a mighty person in prayers. Our tribe has always lived with the truth all of our lives and you have now replaced it with insanity. What do you call that that talks to the wind's ears and get answers from the wind's mouth, and reasons doubting everything he or she sees, hears, touches, smells, or tastes? I call it a lunatic, no more.' Those who were dying listened to his passion and those who were young ignored his craving. Thus, the god of joy would stay in youth forever.

"'<'Yucahu made me a rebel in Father's eyes. I am the lunatic that sees the invisible shape without doubt. Yucahu is the spirit of passion between two lovers. He is the whisper that yearns for passion in lonely nights. He is the flame that makes a woman's cells dash up and down the body with the touch of a man's gentle tracing fingers; and he is the scent of the sparkling water and the taste of my lover's kisses under the spying moon in the azure brine. Oh, I called myself a fool a thousand times!

"'<'My secret escapades hinted a suspicious tribal disloyalty. The fire of rage has been burning steadily for a while in Father's eyes. But the wound to his divinity had made of him a moral mortal; and then, a blow of destiny would assail him again; his daughter, the image of his strength, shattered in his eyes.

"'<'I was with child, then. Though I was happy with conception, a good custom haunted me down. The purpose of the act, preservation of nobility, survival of a dispersed nation, had tied me to a vow of marriage; I was engaged to a good cacique of Caobana; but that tiny flame inside me broke vows and customs, tribal loyalty, nobility and honor. My only refuge was the hug of my lover, and the hope of life.

"'<'A walk through this village showed me the difference of two clans. My father's tribe was dying, and the classic tribe was thriving in Kiskeya.

107

I noticed how, invisible to eyes, blind to feelings, the classic clan had expanded over our land, and conquered all the corners in the five unique chiefdoms. (Now their customs tiptoe graciously over every village of the land. The boys and girls of our clan pursue their habits in our games; our songs are full of classic Taino expressions.) An ancient prophecy claims that a good group of people would shape this part of Kiskeya into a chiefdom, under a corrupt king that would come from the classic clan. My father fears the time has come. The classic tribe has already named this land Jaragua; a land that had no owner since it moved up from the bottom of the sea into this beautiful and generous air. Nonetheless, I saw freedom and happiness in your village. I came here and I wanted to stay, but I couldn't throw this burden on your beautiful place. The other half of this prophecy proclaims that 'through wars and pains will this land be united.' I left in silence, and with a bitter heart I controlled my teenage eagerness.

"'<'But I was with child then. This grievous burden of mine was a curse upon my people! I was trapped in a world of uncertainty. The light air that we breathed pushed hard into my nostrils. A gloom descended from a dark world upon my head and deprived me of sharp reasoning. My heart broke into pieces with the thought of disloyalty and glued back together with the thoughts of my conception and the feeling of a warm embrace from my beloved. Oh, how hard can teenage years be, for decisions are curved and uncertain!

"'<'I was a rebellious teenager then, I was right on every decision before my pregnancy, and Father and Mother's advices seemed chains tied around my ankles. Conception brought me down from the white soft clouds. But confusion brought choices impregnated with uncertainties. Oh, it would have been easier to follow customs in these teenage years than to consider my noble parents as subtle enemies. In the entrance of despair, I could only fathom three choices. I imagined a girl hiking up a rocky cliff and plunging herself into the ocean's mouth; it would have swallowed me into a dark world and fear would have been no more; or I could have run to Father instead and told him that his injudicious girl demoted her rank from nobility to commonality, and brought happiness to her soul and disgrace to his; but fear of his figure loomed in my mind and a thought that he could assume the form of a monster poked a thousand times my heart; or I could have run into the arms of my beloved and advanced this prophesied war that was already happening. I did nothing but stayed lost in thoughts in my private space for twenty five days. Then Yucahu, the soother of souls and master of invention, whispered these words to my ears: 'A mother is a faulty child greatest ally, and this noble woman is a liberal by nature.' Then, as fast as a thought, the mere god grabbed her hands and led her into my private quarter. I ran into her arms and hugged her as tightly as I could; I drained all my sorrow out through my eyes and I told her I was with child.

"'<"'Oh, sanctity of nature, give me peace and wit!'
She fainted and fell to the ground as a gliding leaf
from its tree. Then, she began to breathe slowly and
her heart began to beat normally, and up on her feet
she stood before me. She read into my eyes the
three choices. She had not spoken a word when she
was already preparing a bundle of things for me to
carry. Then she answered briefly: 'Life is sacred.
The war has already started. Run and find him
whose passion awaits something good. Now, the
child you have in your womb is the survival of our
tribe in Kiskeya; protect him with your life. If
madness and uncertainty hunt you, hike up to the
higher mountain near the lake; there is a secret cave,
with rocky upper limit and sandy ground, full of
roses, and open to filtered wind; there any pair can
raise a child healthily. The fertile mountain will
give you fruits and the lake beneath is saturated
with fish. Look at me now for the last time, and
don't forget your roots or we will all perish with
time.' So, destiny has thrown me in search of
Yananini to your village.

"'<'The classic Taino women sang and recited
women poetry. They planned, decided, and acted
accordingly. The path to this village is an extension
of ecstasy. These women, like ours, defended their
customs happily. By now, I was submerged in their
reality. But uncertainty kept tracking me. Finally, I
trusted my instinct and it led me to the house of
Yananini. At first, the hut felt desolate, but the
sound of the yucca grinder revived it. A very very
old lady came up to answer me. She said: 'You're

probably not the girl that Yananini waited for. Well, he left. He took a canoe to Caobana in search of an exiled woman. When he left, he clearly told us that he was gone forever. Be you a friend, look for him here no more, for you will not find him.' I turned my body toward the *caney*, and I walked a short distance and suddenly turned my face back toward the hut and the woman and the hut weren't there.

"'<'I headed back through the *batey* with the bundle on my shoulder. The women seemed all happy there. The children played energetically and joyfully. The men came from the sea with fish or from the field with vegetables and fruits, or from the forest with birds and animals. The first star would soon appear in the heaven and I feared I would have to enter the scary forest and sleep under the moon without my beloved. I wept as I passed by the last hut in the village and I prayed in my mind to Yucahu; I asked him to give me strength. Suddenly I got rid of these thoughts that were more bitter and repugnant than nightmares. I clenched my fists to feel the substance of my body and I laughed lowly in disbelief. Then, the voice of a woman came from a hut; my name was the substance. She ran towards me and kisses and hugs returned my soul to joy. This woman was my best friend, who ran away from my clan and married a Taino man and born his child. I spent a lovely night with them.

"'<'Bajacu tiptoed into the quiet village and the chirping of the awaking birds brought contagious joy. Soon, the burning sphere was above the horizon. By mid-morning the village was filled with sweet songs; hope and peace danced to the happy music of the artisans, the planters, and the gatherers; the fishermen sang in the sea and the hunters in the forest. At night the village breathed freedom and the *areito*, like the heart of passion, fed by a thousand arteries, enriched the soul of every person there.

"'<'The next morning, a third day of happiness, brought a cunning scheme of vengeance. First, I saw two familiar faces, seeming friendly with the local people, who were always willing to show their kindness and good will to strangers. Rumor, a friend at times, at times an enemy, came and whispered in my ears that the spies had many inquiries about a fugitive— or about a sequestered girl. They warned of vengeance.

"'<'My dire offense had my father much offended. An evil gloom, invisible to the happy local people, loomed from every angle of my fantasy. (Now, a man would feel the pain of an insult stronger than an immortal lance in his chest, for he could stand it.) So, my good father, driven my madness and conservatism, hanged an innocent man; he was found in his hut hanging from the ceiling, the blame went to his poor reasoning. How hard could life have been on him that was measured by the length of righteousness and goodness? His reputation sank to the deepest abyss. His wife, shocked and thrown into oblivion, was questioned by reputation itself; were her actions perhaps the culprits? And the next day another man hanged himself from a tree, behind his hut, or so the rumor told. Oh, I thought it was the act of madness! My offense had brought vengeance upon innocent people. Lastly, my friend's virtuous husband hanged from his hut's ceiling. Coincidence was quickly discarded as a cause, invasion made every men arm to the teeth, and only I thought I knew the source of the curse; I couldn't have revealed it. So, I took my bundle and I thanked my host and I headed to the cave in the mountain as my dear mother had advised me.

"'<'The night fell heavy on the earth; the moon appeared as it could in the heaven; everything was up in the air like chance. A person could be as good as a described angel, or he or she could be a devil himself or herself as the classic Tainos say. But now, to me, they were all devils. I ran across the forest with fear inside me. Men were tracking me; I knew. But the strength of Yucahu, hope or life as it was, kept me up on my feet. Awake, I dreamt. Then, I knew I lived in a world of uncertainty. Had Father's soul been so disturbed as to hurt his own daughter? Had Pride taken such a deformed shape to change a man into his opposite? O, fear was then the queen of this forest, where there were no beasts or evil spirits, except the spirits of the beasts inside those mad men chasing me. The cold stars were friendly; the full moon scary; the rustling of the disturbed black birds, like bats in a dark cave, discretely swapped places as we ran across the woods. I didn't know whether the men's intention was to kill me or catch me. I would have stopped and gave them my life, but it was the hope of the new being inside me that encouraged me.

"'<'A man caught up to my pace and I, trained as a savage fighter, confronted him. I wrestled him as well as I could. I was then deposed of my bundle full of precious things; they scattered on the dark ground; food and water spoiled; I was deposed of my god and my goddess. But with the strength of him that I lost, I was able to fight off this evil man and to escape from him. By then the moon and the stars were replaced with the first rays of light of a new day. The chase was more ardent and the rumble of feet was closer to me as I approached a moderate cliff. I began to descend the precipice when a man jumped from behind and landed on my shoulders; we both rolled down the cliff; I landed on my belly, and needless to say, I lost another precious treasure. The other men came down, tied my liberty, and brought my dead soul to my father.

"'<'I woke up from my slumber and I was like a seeming quiet river, whose underneath current is deadly. My mind's tongue was dull and heavy. A villain who prophesied nobility and righteousness had killed a conception I would have called a baby. Yet the mad man tried to justify irrationality; he accused a tyrant of killing a tribe; at the time I couldn't understand his words. He said: 'The tyrant is killing our tribe; my daughter cannot contribute to the cause. What is life good for if our values are redeemed for fantasies? The truth is delicious in the mouth of an adult as well as in the youth. Cut the

114

truth in half and you will have nothing but
deception. My daughter, you are of noble blood,
therefore Yucahu to you is the connection of things
and the understanding of your world, and the world
of fantasy. But who is Yucahu for a common girl?
His name indicates that he is a man. His mother is
Atabey, a super woman who has all the good things
in her possession. Yucahu is a man with braids, so
strong that no man like him is found on the earth;
indeed, he is the master of our thoughtful universe.
Where is Yucahu? The Jaraguan cacique is the
closest to the match, they say. This man is a
deceiver, a tyrant, and soon will make himself the
supreme king of this land. O wretched woman!
Wake up from your sleep. You were born to be free
and this religion has impaled your soul with one
spear.'

"'<'I felt weak. I fainted at his babbling. My quarter
was a prison to my dull mind for a few weeks. My
tongue felt as if it had been cut in a thousand pieces.
A silent scream travelled often my veins; my silence
was like a ceaseless sword pointed at my throat,
poking me to prevent every effort of speaking. One
night my mother guided me outside and the fresh air
infiltrated into my nostrils and I sighed deeply. The
power of the Taino *güira* brought memory and life
back to my mind. And night after night I breathed a
portion of hope, and the memory of that whom I
loved came to me with the sound of the tambour in
the distance. Perilous words from a mad man did
not create grief anymore. By then the cries of death,
by the secret raids, became rarer with my

conjunctive deceit and scrupulous treason. I was
then my father fake ally. Then, the day of revenge
came; this poison raging inside me had my dear
father cornered in his own quarter, a stony knife
pointed at his throat; I could not kill him though,
but I forced him to show me the tongue I carried
here as my trophy. Unforeseeable the outcome, the
man is weak without a woman. This woman's
woundless heart beats and feeds with the sound of
the Taino tambour and the güira. I have convinced
almost all the women of my tribe to join yours in
peace and war. They are not here now, but with
your consent, even though I appear weak for I have
felt the freedom to mourn my child and bleed the
poison out of my veins here, they will come with
the hope of freedom and peace. I am indeed the
strongest ally you have in this region.' She ends
with a sigh.

"'<I am captivated by her loose tongue and her
attractive grace. The woman in her feels at ease in
the comfort of my hut; her gnawing anxiousness
assails her no more. Her lost is gained in half, full in
spirit, and her tribal pride rejuvenates in ours. I
consent without conditions to her requests.

"'<Now, the Great Yagua, the sharer of truths,
seeks alliances in Beata, Saona, and Toeya. He goes
as far as Borikén and Caobana. But Rumor,
breathless without running, worn-out of travelling
without moving one foot, wet in local water,
claiming to have come from Bahamas, Guanahani,
and Caobana, recounts that Hurricane has impaled

the Great Yagua's canoe on a crag near Caobana.
With the chief of chiefs of Jaragua lost at sea, war
in the east and in the west, constant cowardly raids
from within our region, the elderly tired and
divided, Teteyoa rises above my head with
popularity. In a short time, this village that once
was a source of truth, fraternity and sorority, now is
a reflection of weakness. Large families are driven
away with the trident of fear. A common chief calls
himself a cacique in every corner of Jaragua.
Teteyoa and her women are all against me; the
village is against me; they throw shames, lies, and
degradation at my door. I cannot take any more
insults from the people; I drown in melancholy.
Then, Yucahu, soother of grief and mental pains,
makes my tongue heavier; I am now silent and
cannot defend anybody, except my own family.
Yucahu makes me feel the fresh air; I see the blue
and white sky; the god is at my side. Rumor must
have an evil intention. Hurricane could have not
killed my husband, I reason. I take my
impoverished sons and daughters to a secret place,
away from chaos. We wait for my lost husband
there.

"'<Meanwhile, the village, at times, acts like an
unruly child without his mother; at times, a reckless
storm in the ferocious Caribbean sea; or the
sycophant of an instigator with a trident, poking the
nation's mind. Oh, I feel as guilty as a worm trying
to bury its head in dirty mud. Why couldn't I have
listened to the wisest man I know? Rumor, devil or
demon or friend, has me weeping under a palm tree.

He torments me with these words: 'Teteyoa was an unruly child under your watch, a reckless storm under her reigning deeds, and a persistent instigator. Hadn't we already had so many evil zemies, I would have carved an ugly one and stamped it with her name? Her cries and her lamentations were as counterfeit as her pregnancy and her pitiable story. Dark smokes fill the empty sky as I speak. The village burns in every corner. The agonizing cries of children and stubborn creatures end in death. Your greatest enemies are now dispersed throughout Jaragua.' Oh, my cries and lamentations are the purest images of my soul!

""<Three days fly as fast as clouds in a windy day. The wind takes me to the village faster than my own thoughts. I stand among the debris. The hellish looking village still breathes burning smoke and tastes like ancient ashes. Corpses lie on the ground with hands scratching the ground as if they were looking for their own tombs. Local gods and goddesses have survived this holocaust. But hope, which I mistakenly thought was dying, for it can never die, is born again in me.

""<In the distance, familiar canoes enter gentle Jaraguan shores. A man, radiant as a material god, with two eagles, one from the west and one from the south, standing vigilantly on his shoulders, comes with his comrades carrying also royal secrets. As he enters the woods, wretched men and women prostrate on the sides of his path, lamenting his previous departure and warnings. Nonetheless,

he takes hopes out of a bundle and turns bitter
frowns into smiles; that is the power of his presence
and his words. As he enters the path of the dead
village, the wind begins to blow the fresh ashes and
makes a patch of artificial fog. I close my eyes, and
suddenly the wind is pacified and I feel the ashes
falling down like snow. I open my eyes and here is
this man of flesh and blood standing before me. I
am mute, but I have nothing to tell him; he already
knows my errors and he knows the whole story of
his people.

"'<My people, my clan, my nation, open your arms
and receive with your heart the founder of
Yaguana.> A hush falls on the *Batey* and the Great
Yagua's presence lulls their anxious spirits. His
words are soothing; they have been pounded with
threats before; but the Great Yagua turns all threats
into hopes, some hopes into beliefs, and some
beliefs into customs. Oh, how soothing are the
words of him who knows!

"'Yagua leaves the stage, the bonfire is now open to
those who wish to vent their frustrations, or expose
their ideas, influenced by the new firewood in the
blaze. They stop prostrating as the chief walks away
into the caney. There are dances and music and
from time to time someone gets up because he or
she has something to say; the music stops and they
all listen. Some ideas are thoughtful while others
come out of drunkards' mouths. These are some of
their sayings:

"'<Men and women are both animal and spirit. The Tainos are spiritual men and women.>

"'<The woman is created by Yucahu at the same that Yucahu creates the man.>

"'<Taino means good people.>

"'<At time the animal is stronger than the spirit; at time the spirit is stronger than the animal. But, a good person is stronger in spirit.>

"'And the dances and the music go on.

"'<When a people forget, a new culture is born.>

"'<People by nature forget, is it good to remember forever? Or are we by nature to evolve and change our forgetting fabric?>

"'<Memories are not goddesses, but they have created us as we are. Yucahu create our memories and he bestows them as gifts upon us; so we grow naturally with them.>

"'<The seeds of memories are sowed in the minds of our children, and some youths consider them a form of slavery.>

"'And the dances and the music go on.

"'<When memories die, so does the spirit.

Everything with natural memory has a spirit; the bird that leaves her nest and returns with food for her youngsters has one of the purest spirits.>

"'<Here our chief seeks truths and when he finds one, he ties her hands and feet and presents her to the people as a slave, so that they might know her. The Tainos are good people; truth sharing is the best thing we have.>

"'<The truth is something delicious, and he who doesn't share it with others is a glutton because she

clones herself and she is always abundant and the same.>

"'<Yucahu is the truth, is living, and is the spirit of nature. Atabey, the essence, is his mother. Do not share the truth and you will always be at war.>

"'And the dances and the music go on.

"'<The truth is not always tasty in a bitter mind.>

"'<In human life, everything always seems to repeat itself.>

"'<The wind brings tears but it also dries them up.>

"'<This nation grows and talks of peace through war.>

"'<Sometimes a lie cannot be detected, but one can always smell its pungent consequences.>

"'And the dances and the music go on.
"'<When a tyranny is defeated, there's already another one surging on the surface.>

"'<Yucahu doesn't need to think to do something good; he never errs in thinking. He doesn't think like a human for his greatest is unlimited.>

"'<He who dies loses the hope of living in Yucahu.>

"'<My god moves the trees and squeezes the clouds in the heaven.>

"'And the dances and the music go on.

"'<Yucahu doesn't reason, for he is the reason.>

"'<Yucahu has no memory, for he is memory.>

"'<I keep my hope to continue to live in luck; the world of Yucahu.>

"'<To those who seek injustice, give them disgrace and shame and those will be their greatest punishments.>

"'<Long live Jaragua!>

"'<Oh Jaragua, land of paradise, there will never be in the world a nation like you. Your ambitions are few; and your peace is heavenly on this earth. Your charity is incomparable because you always live in the present and day by day Yucahu blesses you with the things that you need.>

"'<Jaragua always thinks in the present; regardless of how much a person thinks, his or her thoughts are always in the present; we can imagine things of the future in the present. Even the images of the past, the famous memories, are in the present.>

"'<Oh Jaragua, land of noble people, you think without malice and live renewed in your precious fortune.>

"'<Good and true ideas create the gods and goddesses; they seem to never die. Our God is with us and in us. If we die, will another godly nation embrace our Yucahu?>

"'And the dances and the music go on until the liquor and the tobacco is gone.

Invasion of Yassika

VII

"'The next day Bajacu descends from the heaven with light rains. The sun fights its way through the grey clouds and its splendor conquers its dominions again. Now, Guatauba tinkers the soles of key men and women, and they wake up with the Great Yagua's radiant presence. One by one, they hear words of loyalty and alliance; all, some in fear and some in grace, venerate the sun.

"'Yaguana dresses with the stripes of war; she dances songs of war. The Great Yagua balances his stripes on his face; they are red, white, and golden.

The other warriors and the drafted mavens repress their envy indulging manners, some by reason, others by fake loyalty, and they smear their faces with one stripe of white for the god, one stripe of red for their blood, and another stripe of white for their goddess.

"'The reason of war surges with confusion in a sea of Nitainos' doubts. Morale crawls on the ground instead of flying above the clouds as the Great Yagua had thought. With Cacibajagua forgotten among the commoners, and eroding from the Nitainos, for the necessity to remember it gives them no advantage, the Great Yagua's origin and his godly royal authority are forsaken in secrecy. But Yucahu, the god of reasoning, puts on the garment of a spy and mingles with the Nitainos. He finds out who is trustworthy and like a gossiper runs quickly towards the Great Yagua, unable to control his tongue, and he warns him that purity and innocence are lost in rational men. Now, the Great Yagua has to find something to offer them in exchange for their loyalty.

"'Hence he tells them this: <Warriors, without you I cannot fight this war. Some say that time has come and eroded my decency. My dignity forced me to bring you into Yaguana to form alliances. But I will not put the safety of this nation at risk, only to accommodate the inconveniences of personal irrational interests. Let it be known now that the sun cannot be the moon, and the moon cannot be the

earth, but they can all live in peace in the vast
universe. My decency should not be in question.
My pride is to share with you my values and a
peaceful Jaragua. Have you no eyes? We will fight
these wars because we are often attacked by savages
from the sea. They plunder our villages and murder
innocent people at will. The aborigines raid our
towns and steal our foods and our household gods.
 Tainos ally with non-Tainos and burn their own
villages. My decency has nothing to do with these
wars.

""<People even question the existence of our god
and our origin. I don't blame them because blind
ages have erased memories from their souls. But
our highest nobility has kept some of them secret
for a long time. Now, think of this, nobody
knows our origin better than us. Nobility is not in
the blood, but in the spirit. Knowledge of our
descent resides in memory, or in our grown spirit.
Cacibajagua is vivid in my mind and dead in yours.
Let's not dig too deep, we might find ancient skulls
and bones of beasts in our backyards. I assure you
we have grown from the ground of Cacibajagua,
anew; blind ages over blind ages by nature can
erase a man's memory and create a better or worse
species; the Taino race was born in Cacibajagua.

""<I cannot fight these wars without you, nor can
you live in peace without winning these wars.
Those who want to follow, follow. Those who want
to dissent, dissent; those who want to value
themselves, have loyalty and valor; we can win this

126

fighting with a few brave men and women.> So ends the chief, and they all follow.

"'Among a remarkable man, strategies and tactics abound. The cacique is the most knowledgeable of all the people in Jaragua; he will come out of his endeavor victoriously. He is the bravest of them all; even the cacique knows his limits, there's nothing he fears. So, among his mavens, he chooses a true behique, knowledgeable of the spirit of nature, for he knows that nature is limitless; nonetheless, he knows that a certain kind of grass can heal a physical wound, and he is also known for his ability to hear the harmony of the wind and the growl of the raging sea. The Great Yagua never thought that this rotten rod, once contrived to be an instrument of peace and justice, enough to keep him at his side, would be a whip of fear, used to turn brave men into cowards. (Oh Jaragua, the remnant of pure men will soon, in ages, disappear!)

"'A remarkable man is always accompanied by a remarkable woman. Her presence feels like that of a goddess when she is at his side. Together, they are adjacent pieces of the same puzzle, the complements of the heart and the brain, the head and the body of one nation; the barren universe can fill itself up with two celestial beings and remain forever one. She is also one of the golden pillars of Jaragua; Kiskeya sings her songs and recites her verses as well; and Kiskeya's deeds are aligned from time to time with her sayings. She possesses a virtuous tongue and an enviable memory. (Oh

Jaragua, how great could you be only if her memories could remain in you forever?!)

"'Deep within the safe and refreshing forest, the great philosopher and his troops stop under the shining stars. A bonfire is ignited and a frame of a barbecue is erected. To the Cacique, the flame of the fire is the only spirit that can be seen. It cracks open the sticks of wood and drain the juice within them like an animal with vicious teeth sucking the blood of its prey and enjoying with gluttonous habit its flesh. If the spirit of the forest is fed, so is the spirit of the tribe. The artists of the güiras and the tambours donate the beats of their instruments, like sticks of wood, to the tribe to keep its blood in flame. The artisans admire the shape of the flame and in their minds think of the shape of the gods and the goddess— the simple vase for water and the cooking pots. The lovers of the stars and the moon construe the truths of the universe and dream of fantasies. The craftsmen see better canoes in the raging ocean and standing huts in the midst of a hurricane. In fine, the poets embrace the warriors, the land, the blood, and the fire. The fire dies or hides and a drunken man gets up in the dark, before the tribe closes its eyes, and he says: <The Origin of the Good People. Blind ages, by the ordinant nature, covered the origin of the forest people. The fire was a gift of nature, the water was a gift found in and on the earth, and the earth contained the genes of the first women.

"'<The forest people had no names; the forest people did not have a god. They threw their dead to the beasts of the forest. They took away the children of others and they didn't cry when theirs were taken away. But they buried not their dead.

"'<Blind ages brought the woman of tears. When her child was born, she was filled with courage. Her child grew up with the genes of her mother. Dignity and pride removed him from others. She buried her father, her mother, and the relatives to her dear.

"'<Then the time came when a mighty empire formed in a faraway mountain. They denied nature, or they saw her with squinting eyes; they became liars, and gave fake powers, (feelings, thoughts, and ideas) to a sphere of fire and rocks that they saw in the heaven.

"'<These senseless people came down from the remote mountain, and they took away the youngsters; the path back was long and sometimes the slaves didn't make it. Their ambition was irrational; their irrationality was called development and human advancement— a senseless imagination.

"'<So, one day the women of tears were tired of fear. Freedom drove them away from the flourishing forest and threw them on the Caribbean shores. Out of tall Amazon trees, they had carved enclosed canoe-like vessels, and they threw themselves in the ocean. The mountain people followed them closely.

"'<Fear returned to them again for they heard the waves of the ocean roaring. They were inside the mouth of an unknown beast, and island by island the savages followed them. Half way to their unknown destination, the strong wind roared louder than the pumas and churned the water of the sea, and hurled the canoe-like vessels to the shores of Kiskeya.

"'<Afraid, yet with some courage left in their hearts, they climbed up the highest mountain of Kiskeya, and hid themselves from the world in a cave that came to be known as Cacibajagua. The ventilated cave protected them from the savages. A small stream flowed with pure water in the cave and they knew, then, that peace was recited in their new house.

"'<The huge cave gave them hope. Birds came to sleep in the cave and they roasted them in gentle fire. They found eatable roots in the upper limit of the cave and they grew stronger together. Then a blind age erased their memories; the old people came to be dust and water. And it was then when a new people emerged in the cave; a new people with a god and a goddess; they called themselves Tainos, the good people.> So ends the voice of a man. And now they all go to sleep until the next morning.

"'Bajacu surprises them all with the twitters of birds. Had the birds been fierce enemies, even the most cautious of them all would have tasted blood out of a stabbed spear in his own heart. But the royal cacique of Jaragua, cunning as the sagest man, for superlatives are not given to him out of curiosity, had walked this wood in intended amorous adventures before; he knows his ground and beforehand he has deemed it safe. Now, whether it be true or fiction, to his understanding a woman would be loyal if she believes that her man, when he is at her proximity, burns inside with carnal desires. He had made secret marriage vows to Anaya, the ex-cacique's daughter of the village they're about to visit. Realization would have come through a contriving alliance. But Anaya's father, quickly overthrown by a mob of power-craving worms, after Rumor had vanished the Great Yagua from the world, is knotted up by a deep depression in a common hut. The beautiful Anaya is harassed by slothful deject suitors, whose competency goes no further than to eat wildlings and whose ambition acts indifferently at their presence; yet, some people call them moral for their desire to marry one and only one noble woman, who has in turn rejected them left and right. Their problem now is that Rumor comes again to stir their minds and it has told them that the Great Yagua will come and slaughter all impostors, and like his brother in Maguana, make alliances by marrying the noblest woman in their town. These 'scrupulous' men envy him even more for he has the strength and godly given power to associate with polygamy. While common men, as they really are, for they can only have secret mental fantasies, praise the honorable and shameless state of monogamy. They now prepare for war.

"'The Great Yagua and his warriors—culture makers—invade the fragile village, where old men, anxious with hyperemic minds, fed up with despotic indolence, idolatrize the warriors as they enter the dusty road of the village. The farmers, hungry and bony, feed themselves with the look of their empty *conucos*; they are unwilling to plant a seed or a root, for when the fruit is ripe or the yucca is fat, they are stripped of their desire to share and the naked futile pride of their work is cold for it feeds injustice. Wedded women stand with their fat-belly children on their hands at the threshold of their timeworn *bohio*. The naked virgins hide at the side of strangers; they feel shame and fears. But unwed Anaya, pure of heart, unchaste under all forms of the moon, proud of her past actions, is invigorated when Guatauba whispers in her ears that a man with strength of spirit and the wisdom of solid reasoning, looking godly, has entered the village with his wife and his warriors. The cowards, rash, reckless, unfounded, and under-confident as they always are, first take inflamed torches to burn a hut here and another there, twice and thrice and more, and then they plunge into their eminent deaths with axes and shameful lances; they all aim at the wrong man, the man protected by the immortal shield of god. In battle, a courageous man is always tainted with the blood of cowards; and so the quick but gory encounter comes to an end, and the passive war begins.

132

"'Anaya stands in the mist at the end of the path; her cheeks are double striped with white, a prudent warrior by nature, and a pious woman by heart. The royal chief, his wife, and his army walk towards her. The path seems long; it is gory, and crying women scatter here and there over the fallible corpses. The eyes of the town are now suspended over the royal chief and his people as they walk on. Then the eyes and ears of the town are left behind as the army meets Anaya in the mist, in the distance. She kneels to venerate the greatness of the chief and the nobility of the queen. Her heart beats normally as she rises. The meaning of his words to her is hidden in symbolism; he mentions the brightest star second to the sun, the mountain and the ocean. The warriors are ordered to scatter away and the queen and cacique stay with Anaya. Then she says: <my chief, my queen, I am your humble servant. I could recount the atrocities befallen here, which Rumor spread and brought you hereafter, but what purpose would it serve to debase this yucayeque even more? Oh chieftain, you have sensed the mere events and foretold me the outcome with such precision that my nerves, visibly, make the temple of my soul tremble at your presence. Your leave began to rot the flesh of the village, but there was strength in its bones, also in me, for you have promised to return and the hope was persistent —but your proclaimed death corrupted the youth and overthrew half-spoiled minds, and my heart began to hurt, for a fault of your own, after you allowed me to deem them stars as big as the sun, I only meant to encourage them, as one should their

133

own, but you knew that their mass was hollow
inside, and therefore they were static commoners.
But all these crafty events, an ingenuity of your
design, purpose had delivered them as said, except
that I don't understand the finale, for you have told
me once: '. . . and out of the dead the vanished one
will come again, as a warrior, and he will enter the
path of the village with a mortal lance, and his wife,
with his support, will rule a utopian village until the
end of her days.' But, sir, the injuries to the village
are too great, the cicatrices are carved too deep, and
it will never walk on its own for its *conucos* are
empty, and the sea seems to be without fish, and
anger is now our consolation. These mothers will
unjustly claim that the toll was much greater than
their son's crimes. The young will grow up with
hatred. My chief, my queen, your reign here will not
be heavenly.>

 "'Now, the cacique, posing as a man of conviction,
speaks to the ladies; his words hide from the
gossiping wind while the cries and the dirges of the
grieving women elevate to their peaks in reaction to
the piling of corpses and familiar faces that are
never to be seen again. Then, the cacique stops his
rhetoric, leaves them alone, and the queen starts to
speak: <Brave Anaya, when Zui and Yaquimo were
two, our fathers, each native to his own land, were
bitter enemies. It was but a marriage of the two
lands that brought a goddess into being and our
fathers became brothers; our sweet and powerful
Zuimaco was their love; she's always been in the
Great Yagua's watch. Jaragua seems to be divided

134

now, but our goddess is one and with her power she will help us conquer. The same strategy is needed here. As a woman I cannot be angrier at your amorous adventures with my husband, a spike inside me is poking my nerves and my heart is beating at different rates; I want to suck in all the air of the earth and see you suffocating. But circumstances hold me. They say it is impossible for a man to love two women, and it is possible for two women to love the same man; but we both know that the Great Yagua is not a common man; he's not a liar, and therefore I think you should honor him with a marriage. As an ambassador I will work with you, but as a woman I ask you to separate this polygamous life from our noble duties.> They hear rumbles and scattered cries here and there. Anaya takes the queen's hand and leads her into the old-looking *caney*, merely a common hut. Her father, crumbled by misfortune and folded by the years, squats down in a corner with his arms around his legs.

"'Then Anaya answers: <Oh, my queen, how came I to be a part of his design? Was it fate? Can a woman believe in such predicament? Or was it a sly contrivance of the man? I am a warrior, my lady, but you don't know the intensity with which I oppose your ignoble desire. I breathe reconciled thoughts and I would share my air with you because I am both a true warrior and a woman. I refute to honor your request, or rather his. Am I an instrument of politics, or am I a woman, or was it my destiny, foreseen by the godly man, to be both?

Who is a liar, he who hides the truth, or just he who uses words to say the opposite of a reality? He never did lie to me. But did he keep you informed of our secret romantic get-together? I feel guilty now, but not of my past felicity; the guilty thing you see in me is drawing out your nobility. Oh, how selfish can a woman in love be when her possession seems to slip away from her fingers even partially? I don't blame you, woman, I recognize this selfishness as a woman's strength. When a woman possesses this feeling, she is willing to follow her man and build a strong and noble empire. I wish I would do the same, for I love him as much as you do, but I think this is your destiny. Who wouldn't bein love with him who's the truest cacique, be he honest or a liar, who has poised as a hummingbird in midair, feeding his spirit on the nectar of two beautiful and noble flowers, and has spoken conviction. Oh, he that comes as the preservative dose of union, commander of an army of sages, soother of cultural pains, conqueror of women's hearts, and the most courageous among the bravest, keeps his vows instant.> The queen goes to the altar and finds Zuimaco. Anaya prepares some juice.

"'The queen replies: <Anaya, now I understand why the hummingbird chooses the best of the flowers to feed on. At least, I give him that. You blush as the mere mention of the man you love, and then I ask you, is it common to feel jealousy? And yes should be your answer. It is noble to recognize one's weakness, but jealousy is not of the noble but of a human. Politic is the best of the policy for it

gives us a mean of survival; what is not noble is to
act incontinently because of jealousy. I am a
woman. I have been in more than twenty weddings
in Maguana already; I have seen women marrying
the same man; and the man is not a common man;
and the women are as happy as the nation; and they
called themselves noble. However, Jaragua has been
a stubborn nation; because our leader has neglected
her and has let her grow unwatched with a purpose.
Borikén and Guanahani consider him a hero. He is
Now within us to forge a good nation. His goal is
not to announce to all a thousand of classifications
or to reveal his state or personal secrets and be
accountable to wife, child, or politician. Maybe,
you're an instrument of politics. Believe me, in
Maguana there are many women who don't know
their husbands as well as you will know yours. He
loves you dearly. He needs you, too. I recognize my
weakness, but I would not act on it. Now, you are
the selfish woman, whose noble man adores her and
is unwilling to compromise to save a nation.
Change your mind, adapt to the politics you hate,
and life will be gracious.>

"'The queen feels a pain in her heart, but she does
not show it. Anaya knows the drill, and she comes
and hugs her deeply. The burden is shared. Then,
the god of contrivance calms their hearts, and hope
(that only breathes in the living) crawls out of their
pores; and freedom sweetens their mouths with
playful laughter. The talk goes on as they now
choose the shapes of the patches to cover all the
injuries and the ointment to erase the cicatrices of

the town, and they also weave the fabric with which Jaragua will dress from now on. So they concoct the poetry and the songs, and the rewards in sports and the beliefs about the stars, including the Great Yagua's plan, and they put them in a *macuto*, like seeds to be distributed in a fertile field, undermining the ingenuity of the man that has brought them together. Perhaps, the women are part of a bigger design and their design within his. Their talk with the chief is personal and the long night is their sole witness. Still, outside the *caney*, burning bodies and the final sobs of distressed mothers succumb to the grievous night.

"'The morning comes with torrential rain and the earth eats away the nutrients from burned sticks of wood and the dust of human bones. The trees of the site will flourish beautifully and the earth will not miss the treads of those who once abandoned her. The sun comes out from the east and a plumed man stands awaiting his entrance—a lance in one hand and his goddess in the other's hand. After greeting his friend, a relief from his soul comes out. Then, alone he enters the sleeping village again.

"'The birds have been chirping on the trees and the duty of men to await and meet the chief has been announced by the beauty, not the fear, of nature. The cacique is the first human to open his mouth to announce it. He says: <Tainos are good people and live at the disposal of good generous nature. Your fight and victory here is a testament to that. You live and are now ready to reward this village with

your greatness. Although we seem to slow, I see people that could have been already with an ax on their hands, cutting the trees for the stubs and frames of the burned huts. The best carpenters, as chosen by nature, stand in front of me right now, instead they prefer to listen to my command than to begin their duty. I thank them for that. There will come a time when warriors will come here and whip our children for thinking like that; and the harmed people will be the ones to reconstruct after the calamity of unfair wars. The custom from now on will be to do your duty as good nature commands; I hope Zuimaco will always remain at my side after this declaration. I got plenty of good friends, including all and every one of you, I think. But as you know, a friend is the only person that can become unfriendly just as friendly animals become unfriendly. Because we are good people, the victorious are the ones to reconstruct as their own expense; for the only rewards we seek is honor and peace.> As he speaks, the carpenters scatter by the village looking for apprentices. Trees begin to fall down and stony saws fall on top of them. Those that are on top of the class listen to the masters of certain techniques to survive the fury of Hurricane. The burned shacks will be constructed accordingly.

"'The Great Yagua continues: <The land has been neglected and maddened she has made bony children. The best farmers, as chosen by nature, are here in Kiskeya, and among those are you. Go teach your children because there has come the time when the earth eats its fruits and bears others, but by

nature it gladly feed from us. So, let this custom
come, give to the earth for she will always give to
you.' And the farmers make the first ceremony on
the field. <If she doesn't feed, she is unwilling to
produce; she is impregnated by the luck of all living
things.> Fruits and vegetables are given as gifts to
the producing earth, the top participant in the food
chain. The fields become *conucos* and careful hands
become rough machines. In days, the small fields
will have common and fair diverse flowers. They
would be abundant in Taino gardens and houses,
and the children will be strong by nature. In days
the custom spreads throughout Kiskeya and
neighboring Taino islands. In days, Zuimaco has
created many beautiful things.

"'The fishermen and the hunters and the craftsmen
and the musicians walk to the sea behind the royal
chief. Canoes are built, races won and lost, and
fishing competitions, in which the prizes of nature
are shared in the nightly bonfire, become
proud duties. The musicians work on the beach and
the fields with their güiras and maracas in the
morning. The bonfire marries at night with their
happiness. The sound is an ointment to the injury of
social injustice. The images of pains are thrown to
oblivion and the good image of happiness shines in
this village and in Yaguana. From now on, the fish
of the brine and the manatees and the sharks and the
birds and the yuccas would be shared once again.

"'Anaya has been avoiding contact with the man of
her dream. His wife has become a strong ally.

Anaya has been given free orchestration of the nation. The *areitos* are designed as she chooses. The Jaraguan songs are heard day and night; life is a celebration. The Great Yagua and his wife recognize that the plan has the contrived shape. The village is on their grasp. So, circumstances become chances. Anaya is held by the gentle hand of Yucahu and driven to the starry forest; meanwhile, the areito is on human fire. The Great Yagua surprises Anaya within the forest, as if by chance, walking aimlessly and blindly. Immediately, she plunges into his arms and the hugs and the kisses and the breath of passion pop out as if the humans were the springs and their creations the flowers. Then, the woman resists the passions of the night, and she pushes gently her man and reminds him of his wife. She says: <A man can't love two women. How can a man love a true princess when he has a true queen? She's one among the beautiful. If I marry you, you would not agree that your love will be cut in half or in pieces like we cut our yuccas and divide the pieces among a crowd. A man can't love two women.>

"'The Great Yagua says: <Are you a man? Is this your reasoning? If your saying is true, then my soul is a liar. Why can't a man like me be in love with two or more women like you? True love, not the cynical love, but the love that keeps a man in the prison of a moment, is by definition in our reality. Am I not the chief of your tribe? Don't I wash your smooth feet and tinkle the fibers of your ardent heart in the pond of your dreams? Were your

141

claims true, that my soul was your only igniter? How many times have I seen your smiling face in this enchanted forest? Don't you dream of me in lonely moments? Are we not temporary half of the other? No other half can make you complete. How many times did I hear similar words from young Anaya; words like these: 'If love were an ocean, let me swim in it if you live in it. Why can't a woman love a man like you?' and I would answer her: 'I have always needed you by my side; isn't Love the glue of this young nation. You are not only in my heart, but also in my mind.' Why can't a man love two women if he did in the past love in that fashion?> Anaya sees the shadow of the queen in the distance and she follows her into the crowd in the *areito;* she hides among friends. The Great Yagua enters the *batey* and hides among a multitude of protectors, or rather protected of him. But the areito goes on as planned. Tonight is the last night the Queen will talk because she must go back to Yaguana with half the troops. The Great Yagua will then be a circular nomad.

"'After the festivities, the queen visits Anaya in her humble hut. The queen says: <Anaya, the time has come when I must part and leave your village. You have been stronger than I thought and have respected me honorably. My time as a warrior has ended now. The days ahead are bluer than yesterday, and my heart, half satisfied, beseeches me to go back to Yaguana. This hut is not up to your eminence, marry the man you love and rule from the caney that we built for you. I will remove

all my personal things and never come uninvited. I am a jealous woman and I cannot travel with my husband to the next Yucayeque. He will need a better poet there, you. You are a noble woman and you see the sprinkles of virtues in the air. Believe in your heart and let the children run freely on the roads. Let the women work the fire in the unceasing clay oven; let them share the *cassava* freely with their families. Let the men collect some fruits and vegetables in the field. Let the young hunt little tasty birds and fish in the open water of the heaven. Let your new family, the town, discuss some beliefs and choose the best. Let your *areito* shine with Taino hymns and Jaraguan anthems and dances. Let that be your legacy here. Your future husband, your cacique, will help you greatly. I will go back to Yaguana now. Marry happily the one you love, it is to you but a small duty. Together we will make of Jaragua the best of nation.> She finishes and then she leaves. The next day begins to shape as the Queen's wishes. The Great Yagua accompanies her back to Yaguana with half the troops.

Anaya: Queen of Alliance

VIII

"'Yassika, Anaya's village, flourishes with the
gossip that the Great Yagua will marry the princess.
The little evil things crawling in the imagined forest
are quenched by the quotidian festivities of Jaragua.
Jaragua lifts the cacique by the air in every little
village he marries. She sounds his name with
echoes wherever he is present. Jaragua is capable to
recognize true virtues, the soul of their cacique. Few
wars reign in Jaragua, except the wars of Jealousy
and that of mistaken pride—enough to shake
Jaragua's nerves and make her very angry. But the
opaqueness of anger reigns in Jaragua at this
moment. The Great Yagua will marry popular
Anaya.

144

"'A victorious skirmish had retained the Great Yagua from Yassika. She waits for him and will embrace him as a hero. The festivities had never stopped since the Great Yagua gave them freedom. And the inebriated dances and the joyful singing over the sound of the güira and the tambour, every night, drink the exact liquor of nature; for the people are high in their enjoyment, and it feels better to them than the down of evil thinking men. The Kiskeyans had all adopted this Yassikan custom: to enjoy with music and dances the beauty of nature.

"'All the faithful warriors of Anaya prostrate at the mere starry entrance of the Jaraguan king. The warriors are captives by their own will; Anaya can count on their loyalty. For ninety nights they have met in the batey and they have sung and danced and married with the women of Yassika. Now, their leader, the Great Yaguanael will marry a Yassikan, too. Unexpectedly he arrives at the Areito when Anaya is about to enter the stage. He is given a dujo and becomes a spectator. The seer sees her beauty, a flick of body language, a presence that warms hearts, and he hears a voice that emboldens and soothes minds. Anaya's eyes, camouflaged in intense flirtation, scan the mere feelings of the chief of chiefs in her land; her hair, thrown down to her waist by smooth nature, black as coal, bright as the diamond, suave as the wind, brings the desire to touch rarity of enchantment. But only the chief of chiefs will touch the decoration of nature in that

145

human cranium for now and forever. At the end of
her dance, she rolls, rises and falls at the feet of her
loyal warriors. Jealousy is the tip of intense interest;
some men constantly and cautiously switch eyes
from Yagua to Anaya, but the chief's main interest
is solely Anaya, peace and joy.

"'A loyal warrior stands behind Anaya and says to
the crowd: <Jaragua starts to grow together, each of
us is Jaragua. Her unexpected loyalty to the Tainos,
a magical spirit which exalts the beautiful nation,
herself a symbol of this beautiful friendship,
manifests itself first in the children, then in the
youngsters, and finally in the wisest; and in an
instant, it has transformed into an expected loyalty.
Anaya from Yassika, fearless commander of
warriors, future queen of Jaragua, lives within us
tonight and forever.>

"'Then the royal voice announces: <by alliances
and more alliances of many Jaragua will be one,>
and the areito goes on for the whole night.

"'Bajacu covers the darkness as if with a blue
blanket. A huge bonfire is built in the center of the
batey. The best reasoned fish of the Caribbean Sea
and a large manatee, cut into pieces, and ready for
the barbecue, drums, maracas, calabash and flutes,
common chants and brave hymns disguise faces.
By the striped color on the faces one can now
recognize an active warrior, a common fisherman or
a master of carpentry. The behique's wardrobe

represents purity; the painted lines on his face are red as human blood. Nitaíno tattoos represent their lineages. Each person, each profession is stained with a symbolic character. The Notion designed by the great chief. Chieftains from all Jaragua arrive at Yassika for the wedding.

"'The chief Yaguanael sees his work in the dance; all symbolic characters parade before him that knows his craft. Then his new wife comes, Anaya, within clouds falling from the sky, and the drum mimics the rhythm of each step of the new queen. The Great Yagua stands to receive her and he opens his arms to embrace peace and beauty. The moment blesses the marriage and the sweet night hides them from curious eyes. The passion goes unnoticed.

"'The last morning of ninety dawns comes with laments and sadness; the Great Yagua must part to another war, for it is said that war is the instrument of peace. The most agile young men and the wisest women join his army. Among the new mixed crowd one can see the distinguished carpenters, the fishermen, the behique, and the new queen; one can easily distinguish the commoners by their work and the Nitainos by their offices; the costumes and the masks of a great celebration are now alive in the minds forever or until the end of days.

"'In the woods a courageous man is also clever and cautious. Yaguanael holds his goddess in his hand during the day and at night she reflects herself in the great celestial bodies. Now, the woods of Kiskeya is a like a paradise without ferocious animals or lethal beings, except for the existence of the worst beast of all, an envious man. To guard himself from the fury of envy, the Great Yagua shares his goddess with the rest of Jaragua. And so from time to time they gather under the sun or under the stars, in the open air, for the goddess of nature needs no temple or even a hermitage to be seen or heard, or smelled, or tasted; for this goes against her own nature; so they appreciate their goddess in time of war.

"'Yaguanael keeps envy in check by sharing his fortune and some of his goddess's secrets. Yet, during the day, the figure of the goddess remains in his hand, and she protects him with a sort of natural magic during the night. There's only one thing he would not share tonight or ever, Anaya, the queen of alliances.

Land and Soul

Disloyalty and Hurricane

IX

"'The Jaraguan warriors remain in the forest under
the Great Yagua's suspicious feeling that Rumor
has reached the village by the sea. Nonetheless, joy
accompanies them day and night and envy cannot
tolerate the present of joy for too long. So, now
weakness disguises itself as confidence and she
deceives the commoners and the Nitainos; only the
chief of chiefs is untouched by the false feeling. He
stands under the influence of eagerness, full with
nobility and shrewdness and he says this to his
warriors: <Confidence, if it is something good,
cannot be a traitor. Do not be deceived by
overconfidence, for if it is something bad, it cannot
even seem virtuous. Confidence is a virtue, so let us
not confuse its shape with its extremes; for to go to

war when peace reigns in the forest is an act of cowardice. Enjoy your days in the forest, let us hide in it for as long as rumor prepares our enemies and let us gain back our modal confidence. We're treading to a village that does not celebrate our traditions and they are very jealous of their own; besides, the smell of the air is not friendly, and Hurricane must be churning the passive water of the sea somewhere else. Again, do not go desperate in being heroes, the ferocious enemies are waiting and sensing bad actions; so let them wait until rumor exhausts itself up and we can enter this unsuited village when its people are less aware.>

"'The dances under the shining moon continue with so many slithering days that some of the warriors, among them the mere brother of the chief of chiefs, convene in secret and conclude that their chief has lost his wit; for he has forgotten their purpose in the forest and his only interests are lust and the dances and the lonely company of his Anaya under the passive moon or under the blue sky. Meanwhile, the other warriors yearn for their own wives and a spiking feeling remind them of their abandoned children. So the Great Yagua's brother takes the lead and defiantly says: <Warriors, what kind of insanity is this, that our chieftain has forgotten about our destiny and spends his days drinking and breathing joyful thoughts while our minds burn with worries and nostalgia? Five days ago, he prophesized that the blue sky would turn black just to keep us here in the forest. Has cowardice made

him mad, and is his madness so contagious that we, sane people, continue to drink from a fountain of lies? Have we no eyes and with eyes and wits caution? We can send spies beyond the border he has measured. He doesn't have to know our intention for it is good and we want to get to the end of this mission.> Half the mob agrees with him and half the mob wants no part of the complot.

"'The chief's brother and a companion tread east in the pathless forest and cross the invisible border and find no Yucayeque nearby—they see just a few huts lit by the full moon—even the seen shacks are scattered here and there. They return and gladly share their findings with the others. Another night goes by and the chief of chiefs takes part in the dance around the bonfire, but his message again calls for patience and inaction. The next night, two more warriors tread south and cross the fabricated border, and they, too, find no yucayeque—they laugh at the few huts scattered here and there; and the next night two go north and the few scattered huts made them glad; they, too, share their findings with the disloyal ones; and the inaction and the patience turn their obedience to overconfidence. At night the chief's brother, angry, with complaints against patience and insults directed at the chief, faces the chieftain and demand quick action. Then, the chieftain faces the mob and tells them: <My warriors, full of displeasure and overconfidence you come to me, yet with haste you demand action. Many of you confuse a simple skill with cowardice.

152

I experience the presence of Guatauba gliding through those trees. The smell of death shatters the Caribbean Sea, and with acute shouts his holy tranquility is disturbed by Boinayel, announcing the presence of Hurricane within days. So hear me now, in the forest, run into the woods! Far from this forming yucayeque! Yucahu is esoteric, but Guatauba is felt in the air. Yucahu is eternal and continuous while we are alive, but Bajacu lives, dies and is born every day; he's the god of dawn. Look at the stars. Aren't they part of Jaragua?! Although some shine above our heads, in a few days we will all be far from the presence of Zuimaco; her celestial bodies will be denied to our eyes. Forest in! Run into caves if you can find one nearby! Besides, the people of this forest are uncontrollable, they will not be tamed as easy as you think; nor war nor words will dominate them; only true and equal alliance can pacify their blood; something you cannot offer them. Believe me, this war was never meant to be the way you have thought it would be; we came here together for protection and to find a man called Betai; in this world there are many proud rebels like him. Dance this night and let tomorrow find you looking for safe haven.> So ends the chief.

"'But less than half remains loyal to the perceptive chief and the Great Yagua recognizes their weakness; the dance he has ordered is now without dancers. The deficiency is noted in his anger, not moderately, the great chief is reduced to common acceptance; but he cages his anger within him. However, there are those who uplift his spirit and without knowing why, they form a chain by holding hands and dance with the professing good chief around the burning fire. Then they follow him to a cave where they coil like frightened dogs in the presence of a standing master. They even feel unconfident and insecure under a strong shelter and under the control of the chief that has never failed them before.

"'Meanwhile, the non-loyalists, with overconfidence, believe themselves to be the victors against the cacique. But they do not realize that Yucahu is a shield against evil and Zuimaco is the protector of the chieftain, an amulet of knowledge. So the blue sky appears in the morning, and Bajacu deceives those who don't know the nature of his spirit, and those who do not hear the weeping of a loving god and the anger of the transient god. Two volunteers dare cross the border and chanting peaceful hymns approach a cluster of rebel huts and a rain of lances and spears sentence them to death for their disobedience to the shrewd chief. The rebels scatter in the forest and the non-loyalists invade the empty pocket of huts and cries of war and death reign in the blue sky; both sides lose blood and faith. The rebels abandon their once peaceful land. Then night comes full of stars and the infidels prepare a bonfire and they dance to quench their fear and they regret the warning of the chief of chiefs, but relentlessly talk about victories and the false prophecies of a drunk chief.

"'In the morning the sun comes out half hidden among the clouds. The infidels are animated, even with a quarter of the mob dead, all ready to invade the next cluster of huts. They enter the unwelcoming territory and again lances lacerate craniums and arrows pierce through hearts while stony axes chop arms and legs and heads; the sun hides thoroughly within the clouds. The rebels hide in the forest and there they reassemble with arrows, bows, spears and stones to defend their pride and their right to live freely. They fight against the warriors with passion under lightning and thunders. During the climax of the battle, Betai (the ideal) and his men run like cowards and hide in the forest, not from Yaguanael's warriors but from the dripping water and the eminent strong winds that are coming. The warriors stay behind, feeling victorious, and they begin to dance under the rain and they chant hymns to the dark air. Suddenly, the fronds of palm trees begin flying and the present evil of Hurricane is felt; his fury is incontinent as the fury of the warriors that are about to die. Hurricane uproots beautiful palm trees; he blows intentionally on a tree and he hurls it against a Taino, crushing and exploding his body. Men fly in the skies replacing the shrewd birds that are now hiding deep within the forest. Some men cling to one another and effortlessly Hurricane makes them collide with others in the sky. The sticks and fronds of empty bohios abound in the sky and canoes and trunks of trees float in the raging sea. Then, like a furious monster, Hurricane scans the area with his humongous eye; he roars by combining the explosive sound of thunders and the sweeping sound of the wind; no men or animals or man-made structure is safe. He destroys all he sees with the fury of three times a thousand furious animals. Only those who are hidden in caves and deep in the forest, with a sense of respect for his power, remain alive. Then, he calms down and Zuimaco, mother of the universe, pacifier of furious beings in her nature, swallows him into thin air and cages him for the moment.

"'As Hurricane's howls die, a cold air, like the chilling air of fear, crawls into the cave where the Great Yagua's loyal warriors tremble with despair. But the chief of chiefs stands at the threshold of the cave and the cold affects him not, for fear is nothing but a friend to him who remains pious in the face of disaster; his goddess remains tight in his hand and Yucahu's vivid in his mind. The dark hours of the night hold slow black clouds and the rain slowly dies out. Frail thunders now and after, a sluggish lightning here and there and a feeble gust bring hope once again to the chief's heart.

"'Zuimaco, the goddess of sleep, makes everyone's eyelids heavy and the chief's sweet and comforting voice whispers a song of hope until all fall asleep without frights; even the chief coils himself around his wife.

"'Bajacu appears in the morning accompanied by little colorful birds. The chieftain and his companions wake up to the beautiful songs of hope.

Quickly, they dash out of the cave like frightened squirrels and the splendid sun welcomes them to a clear day. They look at the perplexed faces of each other and their reaction is to run around the forest and toward the still agitated sea; they look here and there and they see the cold corpses of their ex-comrades and the logs of the *bohios* scattered everywhere; uprooted palm trees on the ground and trees rooted upside down; a shallow water shark, destroyed canoes, fish, arms, known heads and the ugly face of disobedience and impiety. Now all the survivors, after the storm, believe in the words of truth. They all wait for their pious chief to order the piling of the cold bodies and the pieces of bodies thereof, and the cleaning of the field where once shacks stood. The Great Yagua orders them to clean up and to burn all sad things in the field. The day drags itself slowly with the ardent work of the crew and by nightfall the smoke of incinerated remains disappears and a huge bonfire is built where they dance and sing and thank the God and the goddess of Jaragua; out of misery, fake joy is a privilege.

"'The chief says these words to his companions: <My warriors, hear me now, never again will this chief allow disobedience from the people who won my trust; for men are not friends of eternal joy but of transient passion. I had a dream yesterday. Gluttonous beasts invaded Jaragua and ate the fruits of all trees and uprooted all the yuccas in the field; even while they were asleep they grasped for food and all things that were eatable. When they were full, up to their throat, they began to fight against

each other so that the food would crush down and settle tightly in their belly; and then they began to kill each other and to eat one another until only one remained; the last one fell asleep and while he slept he spewed some of the things he ate, and then he began to eat his own arms and his own legs; he bit his lips and even his tongue only to die of hunger. My warriors, today I have a hope; you can call that hope one of my passions. Jaragua will be one. We will build a new yucayeque here, beginning tomorrow, but tonight we will dance and be passionately joyful in the name of our goddess, Zuimaco. Enjoy the night before us.>

Land and Soul

Betai's Procession to Yoboa

X

"'Now, driven by desire, the chief of chiefs builds
new Yucayeques throughout Jaragua and he marries
a good noble woman here and another there.
Jaragua grows and grows and the little dirty wars
across Jaragua are scrubbed by the heroic tales
about his leader and by the dances and the poetry of
the night at the Jaraguan areitos. However, there's
an eminence over which Nature has bestowed all
the true and apparent virtues. The proud Betai,
descendant from Yoboa, but native of Jaragua, and
his clever wife and mother, the infamous Teteyoa,
wander as nomads in the Jaraguan forest. His
displaced comrades, with grief and resentment in
their hearts, have all taken homes throughout

Jaraguan towns. They are chiefs and behiques, good dancers and poets, good artisans and apparent loyal warriors of the Jaraguan cacique; nobody knows their bond to the rebels in the forest. Now that some towns have been destroyed and rebuilt or built anew, the cacique's absolute power gives him the title of demigod; his mother's Zuimaco.

"'Rumor walks throughout Jaragua, his feet solid on the ground and his voice convincing in every ear, that Betai's presence will be felt in the minds of the chief of chiefs and his closest allies; his acts will be as the acts of the main chief of Jaragua, for perhaps a replica of action, from opposite actors, can show an evil deed as clear as when seen from the perspective of the injured ones. So the apocryphal Betai and his loyal friends meet within a cave. He tells them these words: <my comrades, are we to sit idle in the presence of evil and let a people be subjugated by the false strings of new senseless customs? Weren't we happier under the laws of nature? They claim that freedom is a right, but the Great Yagua and his people came and conquered by putting limits called man-made laws and customs into the minds of the limited, and aren't we, rebels as they call us, limitless? Who are these people? Why am I hiding in the forest? Why do I have to wear dirty clothes; those that harm the mind? Why does the cacique wear feathers on his head in a fashion prohibited to commoners? We never lived with a god, or at least the god never had the name of a man. We didn't have to wear feather-holding headbands, for nature made us beings unlike birds.

They claim we are godless people, but they were the ones who invaded our cluster of huts and suggested us to believe in a god of their imagination; they call us impious and worthless; they claim that life is better understood with the understanding of their false god. My comrades, look at the actions of the people in every yucayeque you live; aren't they now more loyal to the cacique than to the god they are told to believe in? It looks to me that the cacique is creating a nation of slaves rather than a nation of free men. We will invade Jaragua from within and we will tell the people of their cacique's intention; Jaragua must be free again.>

"'One of the comrades asks him (or for matter, to her): <How are we to proceed? What weapons are we to use and how will our actions create awareness? The people are fanatical, always wanting a master to tell them what to believe in or what not to believe in. Their chief is a sensational man. The goddess of Jaragua is with him.>

"'And then infamous Teteyoa speaks to the men: <Psychological Chaos first, as Betai thinks, then we will create an illusion; Betai must be in many places at the same time. False Rumor will give him the power to burn and rebuild a hut in the South Village in seconds, and hold a peaceful meeting in the North Village at the same time. They will look for him in the south and he will be in the north; he will be in the west when they would be looking for him in the east. The goddess will be his protector. And

162

the people will be on his side. But we should never hurt a single person.>

"'<But why not? Why does it have to be an illusion, when a sour reality weighs a thousand times the pain, or am I wrong in my estimation?> a warrior asks.

"'<I think you are wrong, my chief,> Teteyoa answers him.

"'<How so?>

"'<Personal experience; the man you want to deceive and to debase could be but the cleverest of Kiskeya.>

"'<I will try it both ways,> another warrior interposes.

"'The princess approaches him and looks into his eyes, and then she says: <My chief, are you blind or deaf or has your heart blocked the sense of trust for the woman who loves you? If you burn the hut of a Nitaino, they will accuse you of burning a hut of the nation; and then rumor will float as if with the swift wind into the ears of the commoners; and it will be the commoners that will judge you as a villain, as a traitor, as a godless man. Trust me now; haven't you learned from the noblest man of this land, even when in your mind he is tyrannical? He burns the huts of the commoners, and with the help of the injured he rebuilds them; then he tells them that the

goddess is with him and will hence protect them; he always ends up like a hero. The chief of chiefs in Jaragua is a pious monster. Oh, what a shame it is that to save a nation a man should turn into a monster first!>

"'A third warrior adds: <I will try it both ways, too. And then I will invent another if I fail. I want a real rebel war. I want to see if his goddess can stop a true rebellion. The Great Yagua is a god in Jaragua, he creates everything. The people deem him so; he is the resemblance of Yucahu. The common people do not understand that Yucahu does not breathe or that his blood does not flow through his illusory heart. Yucahu does not feel and his thinking is not human. For a common person, Yucahu is not life but the god who creates the people as a woman who creates a pie of cassava with her own hands. For a common man, Yucahu is not illusory, he is flesh and bone. Didn't you learn anything from your father? Weren't a thousand warnings enough? The Great Yagua realizes what he does. But can he stop a real rebellion?>

"'Teteyoa dares to answer him: <My chief, it is not the Great Yagua you should fear, but the common people. Unless you steal his goddess, the people will always venerate the chief of chiefs. His goddess is true and the chief of chiefs has the right title because of her.>

"'Then an unknown man runs into the secret assembly. He looks at the chief-less unknown faces and can't construe the figure of a chief, and failing he exclaims to the group: <Betai, Betai! News has come from Yoboa. Your father is very ill and even though you do not share his beliefs and his Taino traditions, he wishes you to come back with your children before death takes him away from this land.>

"'A huge silence descends upon the fragile conspirators. A warrior reacts with these words to his dear master: <Arise woman! Throw your cowardice off your beautiful mind. Take your children, and take them to my parents because Yoboa will welcome you with pleasure. Define Cowardice as staying in Jaragua and dying without giving the enemy a war. By eliminating our simple and true ideas, we will kill our souls. Protecting my family, my soul, and my people is a must. My soul is not a naïve being. Arise woman and go fast to Yoboa, for if an unknown man can enter a sacred ground, what would that man who is the cleverest and who possesses the right title know? Arise woman, and I promise you Yoboa and whatever it might become.>

"'And yet another warrior adds: <Arise woman! Arise and go to the few huts of Yoboa, and make from a cluster of shacks a holy village. Go woman and take your children with you; go now and I promise you a goddess; Zuimaco will come to Yoboa.>

"'Now, the messenger, loyal to the Great Yagua, is surrounded by the power of contrivance, and he thinks that he has become invisible to good eyes. He walks away smoothly through the guarded threshold of the cave, and once in the thickened forest, he dashes like a sudden forgotten thought into a new life.

"'When danger howls, the wisest woman collects the most important things of daily life and she prepares herself to escape it safely; Betai's warriors run into strategic points of the forest to die or to survive with honor. Betai's soul cries as he carries his small children into the uninhabited forest and the tears and the doubts, the regrets and the bitterness of leaving his land silence him; but surprisingly hundreds of people converge in a forked road to accompany the great Teteyoa to the sacred land of Yoboa; so begins the first procession to this holy territory of Maguana. Betai thinks of the chief of chiefs' contrivance and smiles as he sees his beloved mother departing; that is the great gossip running through Jaragua: Yoboa will grow with Jaraguan blood.

"'Meanwhile, Betai is a soul and no more; his wife is the clever Teteyoa.

"'A day passes by like a running cloud through the empty sky. The Great Yagua, his main wife, and a few close friends are feasting in Yaguana's caney. An unknown guard comes running through the protected caney's door and says: <My chieftain! My

chieftain! Betai and his men have invaded the South Yucayeque. They burned two huts and killed one of your allies.> A hush descends into the jovial caney; and after the silence another known guard rushes into the caney and says: <My chief, my good chief, the great Betai is in the North, West, and East. Jaragua loves his wits.> The chief, like every intelligent man, listens, thinks, and then speaks to his company.

"'He says: <Does Betai have a nose to breathe, eyes to see, mouth to eat, ears to hear, how do they look? I have looked for him myself and I have seen him not; I have never seen his head or his body, and yet he is the biggest threat to my heart and to my nation. I know these things about him: Betai the noble, Betai the proud, Betai the magnificent, Betai the brave, Betai the honorable and righteous. Rumor tells me that Betai knows our dances and songs, our customs and all the bad and the good things of our growing culture. He has a Jaraguan heart. But has anybody seen his glorious face? He calls our beliefs lies. But does he know that we are keeping a proximity to the truth, for there are many misconceptions in the world? I've been told he often asks: 'Who are they?' And I would answer him if I could: 'we are an expanding idea.' Now I ask: 'Who is Betai>.

"'The Yaguanan queen answers him: <Betai is the greatest menace of this land. He should not be given equal treatment.>

"'The Cacique continues: <We are not giving him anything. We're searching for a ghost. Where does he hide?>

"'Another trusted warrior rushes into the caney: <My chieftain! My chieftain! I have been told that Betai is running toward Yoboa.>

"'The chief answers him: <But how does he move? Is he a man or is he imaginary? He was in the south a day ago, and the west is three days as far as the middle from where he is now. How does a man move?>

"'His wife takes his comments as a joke and she says: <By feet on land or by a canoe on water, my chief.>

"'Meanwhile, fear runs and creates chaos in every village of Jaragua. There is fire in the land and fire in the hearts of people; although some of it is invisible to some; Jaragua is in a war. The Great Yagua runs through every village and peace sits on top of every town and through the Jaraguan Sea and the lovely starry sky and the sunny days. Then a conciliating rumor approaches Jaragua: Betai and his infamous wife are really travelling to Yoboa; Jaragua is safe.

"'The Great Yagua's voice waters the ears of the people as the morning dew wets the yet to bloom flowers of a good field. Jaragua is worshiped with beautiful words; the dances and the Jaraguan songs adorn her head with peaceful feathers and colorful faces. The propaganda that the original Tainos came from Kiskeya's womb abounds in many poems. They teach children to worship the beautiful Kiskeya, where gold flows in rivers and it is not worshiped. Pride is not confused with humility. All Tainos are proud to live in Kiskeya and in the islands of the Caribbean Sea.

"'While different beliefs flourish in the air, the forest criticizes them all, good or bad, and Teteyoa, the great deceiver contrives a plan of peace. She realizes the power of Zuimaco and the ingenuity of Yucahu.

"'In the forest, heading toward Yoboa, the procession goes slowly. Teteyoa invokes the goddess of Jaragua and joy softens her heart, she feels herself like a classic Taino, just like her own companions. There, under the starry sky, she orders the warriors to build a bonfire and dancing and singing and joy accompany them until sweet sleep, with its light hands, closes their eyes.

"'In the following days, tranquility reigns again in Jaragua. The Great Yagua, after having inspected every village in Jaragua, returns to Yaguana deceived by a false sense of peace. Joy fills the hearts of people throughout Jaragua. A feeling disguises itself as confidence and blinds the Great Yagua, the wisest man in the land of Jaragua. A transient spirit, resembling Guatauba, advises him to chuck out some stress from his mind by removing himself to the mountain edge with Marien. There, something like peace accompanies him. The Great Yagua throws everything into oblivion and is held captive in the prison of two beautiful days.

"'The ingenious and brave plan keeps the Great Yagua off the Jaraguan scene. Teteyoa's loyal friends invade the Yaguana's caney furtively. There are several deadly clashes with the loyal fighters of the Great Yagua. But these warriors, thieves of goddess, tirelessly dismantle everything within the caney; they look in every corner; they dig the ground until finally a warrior touches the goddess, the holy stone, Zuimaco, the goddess of the universe; she is radiant like a diamond and colorful as gold. The warrior opens his arms and lifts the goddess for the others to see her; there Joy appears and the warrior is seen shining like a god, with his open hands, holding the great Zuimaco. Immediately, Rumor, as plan, spreads through Jaragua: Betai has found Zuimaco and is taking her to Yoboa. The goddess is in his favor!

"'Indolence walks in all Jaraguan roads. Without Zuimaco, the goddess of union, Jaragua becomes many. The canoes in the height of the Caribbean Sea, at the blue horizon of Jaragua, once placed there by the great Yaguanael, now rest upside down on the Jaraguan shores. Consequencely, the nights hide Cariban invasions. The Caribs sneak in and loot Jaraguan huts and treasures. Fights abound among good neighbors. There are children lost in the cries of women. Terrible feelings hide in the bodies of men. Men squat and cower in the presence of evil. They even forget the Great Yagua's insisting voice that 'in the absence of a great one, a greater and better man is born'. But instead, the people hope for the return of their good leader and his stolen goddess.

"'Betai, the spirit of a throng of warriors, resents the misconceptions clamping in the hearts of the people, and Yoboa claims the hero in him even more. His destiny is long and unsafe. The group of warriors stops in the forest after tripping over charred human remains, indication that evil spirits haunt the forest of the land. Their appetites become fullness of hate and rage. The edible things they carry are thrown back into the beautiful land. When hunger drives the spirit to the point of death, though willingly, thoughts become comradely and life is appreciated deeply. Thus, Betai gives his loyal warriors another custom; and the idea would expand throughout the islands of the Antilles. The warriors meet with Teteyoa and the procession. The goddess is given to Teteyoa and her power becomes divine. The people kneel at her presence and then, only then, Teteyoa realizes why the chief of chiefs creates customs. But now, all the people in the procession will fast to the land of Yoboa.

"'Meanwhile, the Great Yagua extends a hammock across two trees in the mountains and wrapped in it, a slumber sleep sequesters him. He dreams deeply:

Yucahu denied entry to Bajacu in Jaragua. The sky
is a black cloud that envelops all Jaragua and takes
away the greatness of the moon and the
commovingstars. Guatauba moves with the wind
from the south on all Jaragua. Guatauba appears
before Yaguanael and scares him terribly. The Great
Yagua regrets the occasion and feels a brief grudge
but keeps his hope alive and thanks Yucahu with all
his soul for his protection. Hurricane has visited his
land uninvited three times so far this year. In the
distance, sea waves shake the beautiful Caribbean
beaches. Hurricane is much angrier than before and
as evidence he sends his most furious winds.
Jaragua has never seen the intensity of such
destruction before. Hurricane tosses their canoes
through the air like leaves in a windy fall. His
terrifying roars frighten all Jaragua. The impossible
is seen; thunder seems to be falling apart through
the humongous cloud. Hurricane makes lightning
spears and throws them with all its fury on huts and
palm trees; the dark sky mingles with the water of
the ocean. *Guabance*, his friend goddess, stirs rivers
and lakes and creeks and overflows them; it
destroys all *conucos* in Jaragua. Women flee into
caves; sometimes they are frightened by the surprise
howls of the evil god. For three days Hurricane
paces himself throughout Jaragua. The destruction
is massive. Only the Cacique's Caney remains
intact.

Land and Soul

The Power of Zuimaco

XI

"'Yoboa's grown to maturity, it is Yaguanael who is compelled to recount the moments past in the desolate forest and the first procession from Jaragua to the mere town of Yoboa. In Yoboa, in a crowd of chiefs and their sons he tells them: <Why am I always put in this position, to remember sweet or bitter moments and sweet or bitter endings? I must please an audience with half of my story; the rest is all well-known by others. I had left life, that quasi-unshaped spirit that beats with a normal heart, resting on a hammock, dreaming of peace, feeling it deeply within its complex veins. The forest on the edge of Marien welcomed me pleasantly. Atabey was with me because she is a goddess of all places.

There, the stars tweaked playfully the coquettish night. The moon was part of my landscape. The sloshing flow of a stream accompanied the slight breeze and the sound of green leaves offered a serene beautiful melody to the night. There, I smoked tobacco from my pipe. Suddenly, Yucahu appeared around me; I thought of a thousand good things before Yucahu glided me into sweet sleep.

"'<The next day, Zuimaco gives me another beautiful day. But the night feels heavy, and resting in my hammock, I dream terrible things.

"'<Bajacu brings an evanescent morning; the sun wanders through the woods as if in a hurry. Guatauba fights and temporarily exiles Bajacu from all Jaragua. His divine message is very decipherable. I jump from my hammock and fall on the ground. Hurricane! Hurricane! Again, the evil spirit, more insane than ever, threatens me with death. Thunders torment me; thousands of them are heard in the heaven. I think of my family and my people. If only I could be with them . . .! But can anybody totally understand the gods? I shake my head and I just hope that Yucahu, the god of thoughts, would guide them to safety. I am enveloped in a treacherous mist with thunders and lightening. I evade lightning, flying rocks, and cutting objects. Many plants are halved by strong electric currents. Pieces of sky, frozen segments of clouds fall before my knees; I fall and I rise; I run and I struggle to see the path ahead of me. I am no match against the strength of Hurricane; the winds

of Hurricane hurl me against a large tree—I still
have the strength to stand up and walk away from
the windy hands and again I get up and again
Hurricane lifts me up and tosses me into a small
canyon. I feel safe. Yucahu sees me hurt and gives
me the strength to walk along the creek. The wind
above me howls like a humongous beast. The dry
creek is now my sanctuary. I kneel on the ground
and I kiss it graciously. I don't know where I am
going, but I keep on walking lamely along the
channel. Suddenly, I am stopped by the bleak
churning of water rolling down the creek. The basin
of the creek fills up from underneath and a huge
fountain of water rushes down the stream and
splashes me into a rock and drags me downward
along the river; the fury of the water pities me and
throws me alongside the river—naked and half
alive, with a swollen face, broken arms, legs, and
half a soul—I rest to die alone. For three days I have
no dreams or thoughts, no hopes, no fears. And after
those three days, I hear: 'He's alive! Teteyoa! The
man has been revived.' I can barely see; but my ears
are sharp; I conjecture, from the talks among the
crowd, that I am in the hands of the princess, bound
to Yoboa. Yucahu has disguised me as a commoner
and nobody has recognized me yet. They treat me as
a special guest. I cannot talk, I cannot move my
arms or my legs; I am fed while they are fasting. I
feel humble and I cry; tears roll down my cheeks
while the princess herself clears them up. Within
me, I swear to be a brother to them who have taken
care of me. For now, I am safe and thankful to gods
and men.

""<Zuimaco caresses my body throughout the night. She secretly begins to heal the wounds inside my body and she gives strength to a dying soul. I have come as close to death as some of the pilgrims will come due to their fasting; I already appreciate life for it is a golden gift bestowed on men by the divine grace of a goddess. The multitude of pilgrims thinks my final days are near, that I would never walk or eat with my own hands. A few youngsters come and their ill conversation dies with the reproach of an elder.

""<The old woman gives me water and then says: 'He that lives his final day is not aware of the miserable look on his face. But there's a healthy spirit within you; your eyes sparkle with grace, a sign that the goddess we carry to Yoboa is keeping up that fire within you. The few days left in your soul can be very useful to our survival. Now, hear, you stranger under the shining moon, thrown to die under this lonely tree; I have been entrusted to trust your ignorance of the power of the goddess; in this worn-out *macuto*, worthy of a wretched man like yourself, abandoned-looking by the goddess and his family, hides the goddess of the Jaraguan people. Wear this for our sake, and in return you will have bread, juice and water. If by a chance of nature or a complot of men the princess is assailed, for as yourself might have heard the treasonable words of the youths, never talk or gesture about the existing nature of your possession; your silence could keep you alive.' She leaves me to breathe alone, and again I feel the warm of my goddess.

""<By morning, I feel loved by the nobility. The beautiful princess visits me in the morning and at night; the old woman check on my health from time to time; I am the luckiest commoner, for the princess has taken a liking to my injuries and the old noble woman has made me her confidant; I really knew it was because of my goddess, the most gracious. Now the princess comes and our conversations are long and jovial. I surprise the princess with the struggle of laughter; I gain strength and Zuimaco gives me the power of utterance. My voice, hoarse and tired, amuses the lovely princess. It cannot please her much and she closes my lips with her delicate but well-fitted hands. She tells me: 'I am amazed at the miracle of your recovering; but your voice, that was, perhaps, sweet and noble, cannot sing or utter words with significance. Rest my friend, rest and gain more strength, and perhaps I will someday see you singing or reciting in an *areito*. Or if your hidden love is true, recite silently in your mind, for the goddess you protect could make me dream of your intention.' She jests and walks away. But then I say to her in silence, for my mind is falling in love with the most possible, for to be beside such a lovely woman is to be in love with beauty and mind and possibilities: 'Play with fire, woman, play with fire and I might become fire to play with you under the fiery moon. This goddess of mine is a magnet that draws you towards me, for she has intended fiery moments to intervene between you and me.

"'<'Fear me not, woman, fear not, but do not provoke the fire of a strange goddess, when the warmth of your thoughts and your body is a goddess-like impression of desire. Visit often, woman, for a man that is exposed to such warmth once, can never be cold even in his imagination.'

"'<The mere Goddess is still hiding me under the natural disguise of swollenness and Yucahu has now given me strength, for he is the god of desire. I walk lamely with a powerful raggedy *macuto* on my shoulder. The immobile hiding place of the goddess has now become a dynamic wonder. The princess has now ordered me to remain at her side at all moments, except at night when she sleeps undisturbed. I am a man hated by the nobles and loved by the commoners. Although I am a silent counselor to the princess, some regard me as a dejected man, but little do they know that the goddess, after all, has always been mine.

"'<A turbulent moment shakes the common forest just a day away from Maguanan territory. This is the plan: Ambioryx, trusted men of the princess, speaks with treasonable words: 'Fellows,' he says, 'though this goddess has to me no value, her power seems to be consuming our princess. She no longer talks to us as friends of the same cause; her time is spent in planning ceremonies and giving merits to a statue of stone, a goddess that she attributes the cause of much suffering. But now, how can this woman deny her power? Jaragua kneels at her feet;

179

men are afraid to look at her face without permission. Hundreds of people have stormed from all Jaraguan corners and her invisible shields protect her as if she were a true goddess. She is now called the queen of symbols. I am to steal the goddess and to return with her to Yaguana. Those of you who feel my pain or my concern, help me in my risky endeavor, and I will give you power you have not fathomed in your life.' And the thoughts of men are diverse; some see the power of the goddess and some see the evil of greed.

""<So comes the dark hour: the sublime music of the night tucks people into their hammocks or their straw beds and in the dark a hand probes the pockets and the bundles of the nobles and the affluent personalities with no results. Then, anger comes and fire reigns in straw beds and tents and flesh. There's a great commotion and the princess flees from her attackers; her bodyguards protect her and some loyal men follow the perpetrators with deadly lances on their hands. But the princess, herself an agile warrior, runs and catches him that is the leader, and while she has him on his knees, a lance thrown with accuracy struck near his heart and another on his belly; the princess screams in anger. The mob of loyalists approaches the dying man; they show no pity for his crime is treason. Now, the princess scolds those you want to see him suffering and she orders them to give him a quick death. She leaves the sight, but the loyalists stab

lances in Ambioryx's chest and they take his heart out and bury it; they throw his body deep within the forest.

"'<The princess is angry with the actions of both her men and Ambioryx's. The murmur of disgust follows the crowd and the princess toward Yoboa. Her trusted people, her closest friends, are pulled along with her by the haste of the moment. For friendship does not have the essence of a god, it rusts and leaks and it can become the opposite of its existence. When friendship mingles with envy, the closest friend could be a person's worst enemy. So the princess takes her closest friends quickly to the border with Yoboa, and just before they enter Maguanan territory, she teaches them a lesson. I am left behind with my goddess and I can see that envy moves as smooth as a snake within the crowd; she is darker than the moonless night; she makes people trip on small pebbles and big stones. The power of the goddess is envied, too; every greedy soul wants the statuette. Teteyoa wants to show her trusted people that the goddess they seek is nothing but a shaped stone and therefore her power is imaginary. So, the gossip spreads the deeds; I am told by the elder woman the whole spectacle. She says: 'My mistress scolded them all, her voice sounded like the thunder of the angry god of storms. She coached a few men and gave them verses to recite. Then she headed toward a dying tree, pretending, symbolically, to hold the goddess of Jaragua in her hand, and she dug out dirt and interred the goddess under the agonizing tree. A trained voice yelled:

'you know the symbol!' My mistress knows many symbols. The tree where she hides the goddess is not prolific and should not bear healthy fruits. The idea is rudimentary, she said to us: 'if the tree talks to a person, it would certainly mean that a goddess inhabits within it.' So a fake behique, versed in the tactics of the mind and of nature, emerged with three spectators to the holy sight. The symbol of interring the goddess is not understood for the spectators are but common people; so they believed the deed was true. An undisclosed man in the show shook the dying tree from behind. A liar, hidden within the forest, announced these words: 'Cut me by the trunk and take me home for I am the god of falsehood.' Then, the behique examined the trunk and he hesitated before he classified it as a god or as a goddess or as a demon. Then the artist carved the new god's or demon's face with the face of an angry or horrified monkey; it will be shown on the altar of the gods and goddesses and demons.'

"'<On the next day, we enter Maguanan territory. My eyes and my Jaraguan heart feel the differences. The Nitainos here talk like common Jaraguan people. The dimensions of the huts are smaller than those in Yaguana. Yoboa, a cluster of small huts and humble people! The people prostrate at the entrance of the princess. The gossip that she brings a goddess and that she will make of this small village a holy land is welcomed with pride and devotion. (Oh Yoboa, your land gives Kiskeya a hope of unison!)

"'<The first days in Yoboa arrive with smiles and joys. Gifts come from all parts of Maguana. The mere Naca pays a quick visit to Yoboa. His brotherly blood attracts me toward him. But a guard pushes me away violently because my image is considered common. Teteyoa receives the great chief and he allows her to work her unimportant magic in Yoboa. At the moment, the insignificant town poses no grandeur.

"'<But the days make of Yoboa a beautiful place. On a spacious piece of land hands shape a *batey* and pilgrims play the national game of Kiskeya. It is played in the name of peace, blessed by the beautiful and loved Teteyoa. But even Teteyoa who is known for her heart of stone has come to a holy place, for she weeps at night and her heart feels lonely and has irregular beats. A diverse place of holiness is a battleground.

"'<Once in a lonely night, the beautiful bride of the night, looking like a goddess, completely lit by a torch of bravery, faithfully and courageously defies the aaaah of death in the forest. The gold statuette, originally from Cacibajagua, waves a heavenly invisible light upon me. The power is immense. The invisible power acts as a protective layer beneath the hut; no evil man or woman thinks of looking for the precious stone in my possession. Envious and ambitious spears have attempted against her life again, and she has now come to see me well. Occasionally one can still hear the aaaah of death in the forest; irrational and rational beings die for

whatever are their causes. I am now more than a warrior; I feel I should upgrade myself and be a general.

""<Atabey disguises me with a tired face, but my black hair is already starting to shine.

""<Yucahu gives me the words and by divine command the woman gives me her confidence. I'm already the most consulted among her advisers. But love, oh love that cripples the sense of men and women, ties me with illusions. But first, I must hear the things she wants to say and say the things she wants to hear.

""<She tells me: 'False rumors tell that the Great Yagua wanders in the heavens, looking for his stolen goddess. He has contributed customs that ought to be chained, for if they are left loose, they will look for advantages and they will cause great pains.

""<'Oh, wretched and poor man, has this goddess blessed you such that even I come to your quarter to ask for divine advice? The precious stone that you hide, the one that they call a goddess, has placed a burden upon my soul. Jaragua suffers, now without a cacique and his goddess, they say; Jaragua is nothing but a hell. The weak desire not peace and the rich never stop seeking antagonistic opportunity. The poor and the humble think of peace as the most valuable possession; it is the most desirable thing in their world; while for the evil ones, peace is nothing but unprofitable. However, people only seek treasure when they are not satisfied by their riches. Jaragua, they say, is at war. But when hasn't she been fighting?

"<'A warrior exists in wars, a peace maker ends wars. A peace maker can only make peace out of wars; while a warrior cannot exist in peaceful time. Aren't Jaraguan perpetual warriors?

""<'A poor is always fighting to survive; he is in a constant war. A humble man lives in a half-proud society, always humiliating himself. A humble man is a warrior, always fighting not to become an animal. So the game of life must be played by warriors and humble people, for those who lose must bow to the winners and those who win know that they must play again in the near future. They mistakenly blame me for causing a terrible thing in Jaragua. What should I do with the suppliant plead to return her goddess to her missing master?'

""<And I say to her: 'At some point you will have to let her go, but not before you build what we shall call <The Great Yoboa>. So, Princess, you should know that Excellence abounds here in Kiskeya; let's rebuild Yoboa here in Kiskeya to keep it sacred; let's make it like a Batú ball and throw it in the middle of thousands and thousands of Taino hands.

""<'Let's give Kiskeyans symbols in the areitos, teaching them true tales with clear messages. Let them make their zemies of stone and wood, maybe then they will understand that the gods and the goddess cannot have a human voice; they don't talk like us; for talking is a human quality.

"'<'Let us build Yoboa from a simple symbolic hut to the creation of a just idea. Let actions speak for themselves! Hopefully they will say good and noble things. After Yoboa becomes our biggest ceremonial center, let's prepare together the most magnificent of the *areitos*. Let us see the rising of the first Taino sticks dance; let its message be also clear! Let women and men take turn to play and dance in the Taino dance—difficult to imitate, full of contentment; rhythmically unequal.

"'<'Let it extend from sunset until the end of the Batú game, until the moon or a midnight star stands in the middle of the heaven, indicating a true middle. Then, let us conclude the event with a resonant voice that clearly exclaims: <We rejoice in the best of the heavens!> for it is nothing but the truth.'

"'<Then the conjunct ideas of union and peace and fire and desire appease the blaming tendency and the act of unjust war. Just as the minutes orbit into an hour and the hours grow into a day the cluster of humble huts becomes the town of Yoboa. And Yoboa invites Jaraguan poets, and the pious artisans from Magua; from the sea of Higüey canoe paddlers are seen in Maguanan water and from Marien fanatic false behiques and pious men and women.

(Oh Yoboa, no remnant of physical structures will ever tell of the pious beliefs shared by your visitors, for it was all consumed by the souls of religious men and women!)

"'<Meanwhile, the days pass and I'm changing and changing fast. Zuimaco is regained in my mind, and Yucahu, the god of thoughts, gives me the idea of seducing with nice words the woman I want to make a queen. It is difficult to find words to describe completely a beautiful and happy woman, for there isn't such thing on earth; but now Teteyoa is the closest thing to the idea of perfection. My eyes glow when I look at the perfection of her majestic athletic body. That *Taino* woman can climb a mountain without scratching a fingernail. She crosses a river from side to side when the current is high. She walks on rough terrain, from *yucayeque* to *yucayeque*, to recite good poems in an areito. A goddess cannot be shaped, but if I could, I would say that Teteyoa's face is that of a goddess. I cannot describe her perfect nose; her lips are the poppy and the clover; her eyes hide tenderness and wisdom. Her bust is vain for it shows twin sine hills in the distance. Happy is he who stands in the horizon to admire this scene. Her heart is treacherous with the enemy and amicable with her friends. In all, who wouldn't want to seduce her! What man would not want to seduce her! Oh, some might say that for a woman a king might neglect a nation, but I say that for a woman, a man might never deny its sacred birth! My sports with the princess are those mentioned and no more.

"'<Rumor keeps the hope of my existence alive. Jaragua wishes me well and waits for my return. But I have now a princess to conquer and a goddess to keep from evil hands. So, a good day is sent by the god of miracles and I am led by the gentle hands of a soft and fresh breeze into the calm forest. Teteyoa leaves her *Caney* to walk in the pathless forest. Thousands and thousands of blue, red, and green birds fly above the princess; the scene shapes like the scene of the story I want to invent. I walk on one path and she walks on another, towards the same direction, where trees have never been touched by the hands of humans; where a hidden small and crystalline waterfall descends into a sky-blue pond; and across the pond, a man on one side and a woman on another; our eyes' arts meet, and my voice ripples smoothly across the water: 'Teteyoa, Teteyoa, I am not the man you think I am; my goddess cannot hide me from you anymore. My god has promised you this foreign and powerful land and I cannot leave it now without a strong alliance. I cannot promise you a caney in Jaragua for Rumor has it that you are the culprit of all her godless sins and pains. The cures to all evils are love, a wedding, and a common child. Yoboa and Jaragua must be married for the sake of my love for you, my princess, and for the sake of peace, my warrior woman.'

"'<And then, words lose their meanings and questions lose their sense; it is only the magic of the moment and the passion of two who define beauty. Soon enough, two hearts ache willingly and beat

rapidly causing the actions of diving, swimming, hugging, and kissing in a sky-blue virgin pond; we sweat in the fresh water; and the ripples move wildly towards the edge of the pond and the splashes of the waterfall sound like the moans of an ecstatic woman. Then we lie on the bank on the pond, and the land and the flora free my soul even more. My kisses venture over the hills of the land and I kiss passionately the poppy and the clover. Now the princess is astonished by the power of my goddess; in the course of kissing, my hair grows beautifully; the wounds in my body heal completely; my wrinkled and old face rejuvenates; my pleasures and pains are conquered for the moments.

"'<The moments of good life are gone as quick as a sweet wind and a nightmare is as eternal as reality— months in moments—my dreams are sweet and bitter. I experienced first the moments of the beautiful day and then the horrid gossips of Jaragua. My love, greater love, how could I ever neglect you for the pleasure of pleasures! Any man would; but not I; even when I am desirous of pleasure, I always keep you in my mind.

"'<Yoboa, the power of the invisible power, the king of the land, the most powerful of all kings in Kiskeya, armed to the teeth, with lances and love, comes to embrace me as the gossips reveal that I am the great cacique of Jaragua. And I have no shield to protect me, no injury to obscure me, no pain to show! I thank God and my goddess that he

is my true brother. It turns out that the kissing and the hugs are long and prolonged with the arts of the eyes and hearts. My brother is my brother. In a moment, Jaragua knows I am alive!

""<My main wife, the daughter of Jaragua, the love of my love, the beauty of beauties, comes to Anaya, as humble as anyone can be, the queen of my land kneels at her side and says: 'Anaya, your youth has brought me to you, but my thinking knew that you were apt to the art of listening, though I feel weak to speak these words, I know that your love for this nation, as you have once secretly confessed me, can conquer hearts, and an army of Jaraguan soldiers is now at your disposition. You know the gossips and the truth foretold, the fragile nation without a true cacique is nothing but the chaos we are experiencing. Our husband wedded a spider in the forest, and her strings keep him from coming back to his people. Her poisonous tongue, a deadly weapon, can neutralize your nerves or kill a whole nation. We must keep her from our hopeful land; we must not let her shape our destiny with her evil sayings. Go to Yoboa, your husband is blinded by the days of a year. His new wife is with child; a prophecy, perhaps a senseless vision in the cacique's mind, claims one of her descendants, which his majestic has named and by name he has called him 'H', will be one of those worthy of defending our heritage; though he claims: 'In the years to come'. What did he mean by this? I fear his meaning. We both know who our cacique is. His prophecy he will shape truly. I trust in your

judgment to solve our problem and bring our husband back to his land.'

"'<Anaya answers her: 'But has our husband gone mad? Isn't Teteyoa Betai's wife?'

"'<She responds: 'Oh dear, has not the news come to you yet? Has not this symbol haunted you day and night as it has haunted me? What does the mere word 'Betai' mean to you?

"'<Then Anaya: 'It means 'good man'.'

"'<The queen of Yaguana replies: 'A good man is he who defends a nation, Betai, Teteyoa's husband. Allow me to tell you this secret; it came to me in a dream. I . . .' She reveals her dream. A hush descends over the *caney* as the queen leaves Anaya's presence. And magically Jaragua breathes and she begins to heal over all the impatient insults and little wars and hopelessness.

"'<Anaya, the queen of restoration, calls for an urgent gathering of her beloved councils and tells them: 'My loyal men and women, this type of reunion has become a demanding norm, to summon our minds from our daily sweet or bitter dreams at night, and to conspire with the night, to celebrate our agreement during daylight. Sometimes I wonder which life is better, a commoner's or a Nitaino's; for we, true nobles, sleep little just to find the pleasure of some contrivance that could easily be a failure; and true commoners sleep sweetly or

bitterly through the normal night. Our cacique, they say, is a prisoner of a hypocrite queen, a queen made out of denying the true character of human nature; although she denied our goddess and opposed the making of new customs, condemning their plausible danger, she is now called the queen of inventions and the queen of religious innovations. Happy is that queen, captor of our prince and our goddess! Happy is that queen, shaper of our games and sayings! Unhappy is the cacique, unless he rejoices in the suffering of Jaraguans in silence! Unhappy is the cacique unless the woman is an instrument of his desire! Be it one or the other, we must spy upon the doings of Yoboa and then conspire against the queen of inventions.'

"'<The queen expects a noble contribution from her councils. It is the highest ranked Nitaino, a woman that has been a hugger of my own ideas and in her heart a lover of Kiskeya, who stands up and says: 'I would offer my soul and heart to save this nation. I am an experienced midwife and I can serve two purposes: I could poison a spider and cure a nation. Now, I am a true Kiskeyan, and rumor has wandered in our hardship; our king is no prisoner of destiny. Destiny has made him king of this land. Kiskeya is growing and our king is a culture maker. It is no surprise to me that Yoboa is growing in his presence. Pilgrimages from the five chiefdoms are constant in Yoboa, and contributing visitors, from Borikén and other close brotherhoods and realms, with pretty gifts and love and culture are welcomed there, now. I refuse to doubt my cacique once more;

I cannot doubt him that has always been so true. But I also cannot doubt him that has been enslaved for a true cause. I cannot but remember the words of my loyal king, he that said once to his goddess: 'I will protect myself from my enemies, for you have made us combatants in a hypocrite world. I will always, even in the darkest of moment, stand firm like a palm tree, tall and uneasily shaken, to look over the shoulders of my people.' So I say to you, my cacique might be acting according to his beliefs. Be a hypocrite if the end of your action is the common good of your nation. My queen, command this old lady, and I will walk to Yoboa and be a faithful subject of the truth.'

"'<The queen gets up and says: 'Do you think I would have called this assembly if I didn't believe in you, who believe in him, him whom has showed you love and ingrained trust in your heart? What would it be of this hypocrite world if I didn't believe in him that sings hundreds of true songs with different tunes and with the same energy? If I didn't believe in the hearts of the people of this wood; if I didn't believe in him that told me that in this wood, peace is a need, and a warrior like me is the survivor of his creed; if I didn't believe in victory and loss; if I didn't believe that everyone in the middle thinks to be the best, when the best of each kind are in the good extreme; if I didn't believe that war is a natural thing among humans; if I didn't believe that my own silence, although it causes me to suffer, is good for the common people; what would be of this hypocrite world without the

talent of Teteyoa? I tell these things to you: it would be nothing but the vain voice of a poet; it would be a mixture of boredom and inactivity, or a mixture of suffering and suffering; it would be a theatrical scene for a dull play; what would it be of this hypocrite world without Teteyoa? It would nothing more than the clapping of a traitor without audience; it would be nothing but a world of false gods and goddesses; it would be nothing but dullness or misery. If I didn't believe in the sweetest of thing, I would have not called you here. If I didn't believe in the purest thing, what would it be of this hypocrite world? If I didn't believe in the things I hide, what would it be of the trust you have given me through the years?'

"'<And another one of the elderly stands up from the ground and says: 'Perhaps my old age has made me weak, but I think that a pardon and a lesson are more everlasting remedies than poisoning and a deception. What about pity? Where has it gone? Are we to find out the truth and proceed to poison a player, just because she is a hypocrite, or an earthling? I call pity and love to stand up as judges of our actions and dreams.'

"'<And the queen says: '. . . and our actions and dreams are gone without our king; and didn't we once agree that pity can dress that who is naked of evil doing and keeps a promise of cleanliness. Be she cleansed, or be she as evil as a mad monkey, it is not the time to let a belief of righteousness destroy our great Jaragua. I, myself, an influenced

guilty thing, will hide among the servants of the best midwife of this land, hoping that the king will see her in an *areito*; and since she has delivered most of his sons and daughters, he will embrace her as a miracle, as a god-sent angel from a dream in heaven, and she will deliver his son or daughter, and we must be sure that Teteyoa's heart be left without beats. Her son or her daughter will live because his father once told me of a prophecy I cannot deny; (the task I have been given tonight.) Since she must be poisoned, it is poison we will give her. And for those of you who are curious, this is the end of his saying: '. . . for our sons and daughters and their descendants, thereof, can keep a beautiful nation growing.''

""<Another elderly continues: 'Oh, mistress, my heart is weak, but my mind is as strong as a rock, yet I cannot see the benefit of this new endeavor. You are here as protected as the living thing in a clam, and your soul is considered as pure as the sun's light. What else can be missing in you? This endeavor is as dangerous as the unshielded burning sun to a human body. Let things unfold as god wishes them. We must only act aversely to the danger they bring to us here. Isn't it natural for people to have wars and conflicts? Verbal, mental, physical? And after the war, they seem to regroup and they follow what they think is right until they fall in a pit of war again. My mistress, think of the consequences of failure; you are dealing with the smartest people of this realm.'

"'<The queen answers him: 'My lord, idleness is not an option among nobles. Physical death should not be feared, it is a prophesized idea that will invade us. We must act, for what is a good or a bad thought without an action? I would rather believe in my thoughts than in my inactions.' As she finishes her sentence, a rumble of steps and shouts is heard within the batey; and then shouts of friendship fill every bubble of air in the space, and they explode with laughter as it is known that the king of Maguana is visiting Jaragua, and Yassika's friendly warm, since she is in the path to Yaguana, has drawn the king to her consenting arms. Now, the king enters the *caney* and to his surprise, as surprises for a leader like himself are also new but unmoving, he finds fervent torches on the hands of servants and beating hearts hidden in noble chests. Anaya bows at her husband's brother and his army, and then says: 'Naca! This is a most unexpected visit. You are truly welcome here. Have you been an enemy, you would have met the most trained voices of this realm, and this night would have given you an extension of your chiefdom. Come and join us in this seeming peaceful night.'

"'<The Maguanan cacique says: 'I see you are in council. I must apologize for my intrusion, and I hope your urgent matters have been well debated. I was about to camp outside of Yassika and I was reminded of her warm arms, and the mixture of happiness, hope, and friendship promised to me by my brother and your highness in this heaven;

though I hear that Jaragua is not very friendly these days.'

"'<The queen interposes: 'May I inquire of the content of your urgent visit?'

"'<'Yes, it should be a concern of yours, too. I am in my way to Yaguana. For a very simple reason: Yoboa is the largest ceremonial center in the Caribbean Sea now. Even devotees from Borikén and Caobana visit the beautiful Yoboa. The gods are praised there by people from Jarabacoa. The festivities are all coordinated well for all I know. The great chief of Maguana is a god and a tyrant there; I am truly threatened by this indirect menace. They even say Maguanan people are afraid of his majestic presence; a lie indeed; I would say I am rather respected. Yet, I let foreigners wander as swarms of free persons in my land. I, myself, a witness to insults, saw free people rant. I realize that sometimes the virtues are not so far away from people, and they see clearly injustice. Maguana stands and always is very attentive to all complaints of injustice. But we as a people cannot allow a public place to exclude our Apito from a public altar.

"'<'Besides, Yoboa is in Maguanan territory and my Nitaino resides there without power. Worst, that reckless insensitive charlatan, prophet of evil, inventor of calamity and partial truth that we call rumor has created a nest there. Like a spider the monster lays hundreds of eggs that hatch with a good rate of success, and it attests that my brother, my noble and good brother, is behind the tremendous growth and reputation of Yoboa. Rumor even says that my brother intends to stay with his new wife and goddess there. It implies eternal war between two brothers and two nations.'

""<The queen says: 'This madness has to stop now. The humble and the weak cannot withstand a heavier war here in Jaragua. War that is sometimes a blessing and sometimes an evil would feel like the latter. You, my loyal ally, my husband's brother, should know that Apito and Zuimaco find celestial pleasure in Yoboa, and that perhaps it is the only place where rumor claims to have seen them hugging; I also have my spies there. Yet, Apito is not lost; Zuimaco is thought to be away from home. The humble, weak, and poor implore her return for the sake of peace and hope.'

""<Then Naca answers: 'Then, peace is a good thing to the humble and weak, and if a piece of Stone brings that peace, for the people believe that the presence of their goddess spreads life upon the town, shouldn't that goddess be returned to her land for the sake of peace? Think, my noble queen, think, your saying is true. The power of the goddess is real—she, more than anybody must return to her people. I promise you I will support you in anything.'

""<The queen thanks him and continues: 'What about the prophecy, your highness?'

"'<Naca looks surprised at the seriousness of the frown in her face. He is even surprised at the frown of his own face, for it is reflected in the image of a thought. He says: 'Rumor can sometimes hint at the truth, and sometimes it just misses it completely; but how can rumor penetrate one's mind? I had a dream yesterday, a dream I have not revealed to no one, and in that dream came to me a sweet voice with a horrible warning. A prophecy! Indeed, it must have been! But how came you to know about this recent secret? It woke me up and wailed in my head; it put me on my feet and it had me barking to the wind. How came you to know about this prophecy?'

"'<'Your highness, I was just visited by the queen of Yaguana. I sensed a distress so similar to hers in your angriness that my mind saw in you a hidden prophecy; I fear it is the same as the queen's.' The cacique of Maguana asks for an audience to his tale and it is granted.

"'<He tells them the same predicaments and the same dream as the queen's: 'In this life of ends and beginnings, or beginnings and ends, nothing is guaranteed but the A and the Z. A living thing can spring in a moment and shrink to oblivion just as quick. Isn't that enough evidence that the goddess of Jaragua has no favorite? How come the son of Jaragua has now become the only son of Zuimaco? Isn't Zuimaco more than the molding of a human face, the experiences of the eye and the mind, the

subtlety and quietude of the wind, the violent waves of the sea; and the particles of undefined things? How then is a man the image of the goddess or the god? Here is my dream:

"'<'A great foreign governor of Kiskeya stands on the small hill facing Yoboa, unknown by the town in its golden age. Strange beasts, his armed companions, holler behind the invader; but the man himself is the honey-making bee, the cold-blooded shark of the brine, and the leopard of the heat. He brings his comedy to Yoboa. He sniffs; then he chuckles, evil echoes behind him, and the non-existing wolves in the woods hasten them to the safe haven of Yoboa. The compassionate and sagacious Yoboa opens her arms to the strange beings; and people here recognize hungry men or beasts from a far distance. As they walk closer to the town, they disguise themselves as pious and true sponsors of goodness. Even though they babble and hiss as they try to speak, the natives here treat them as humans. They offer them the little food they have gathered for the week, and the gluttonous men devour all of it to half-satisfaction. The Yoboans, shocked at their eating habit or need, pity them and think that it is their costumes, neatly designed vestments, never seen in Yoboa, that make them sweat and hungry. So they curiously approach the strange creatures and they touch with amazement the fabric they wear. But the strangers grunt and snarl at them, and they bow to pacify the creatures, who in turn believe that the Yoboans have mistaken them by gods or angels.

"'<'One of the strangers murmurs: 'I think they think we are gods.' The Yoboans retreat as the howls and growls are the murmurs of the strangers. The strangers roar like the wild beasts in the stories of the foreigners that had been previously swept by the waves of the sea and landed in Kiskeya. The strangers bellow and woof and shout human words to the stunned hosts. Then the aliens see the shining stones, worthless to the humans of Yoboa; the molded golden pebble that ignites fury in the beast hangs in a collar of an innocent girl and in a *guanin*, a lucky bracelet, made unlucky by the ambition of a beast. One of the strange men approaches the girl and kneels on the ground, kissing the stone as if the stone is a magical amulet or a higher god. He kisses her hand and kisses the necklace with the stone; he scratches it with his invigorated paws and then he begins to cry; he raises his hand to the heaven and he thanks his god for his new fortune. Suddenly, he begins to sob as he sheds tears and his heart thumps, and then he laughs as if he has gone insane. He inhales and exhales pains and he laughs again. His joy contaminates his companions. Abruptly, a cruel idea, laughable in Yoboa, immerges in the world. Their priest, gifted with sweet words that carry lies and power, false ideas well-debated among the nobles of Yoboa, rushes into the amazed common crowd; he says: 'Our god, the father of the universe, accompanies us in this very moment. O, father, help us in our new endeavor and help us introduce you, great father, to these impious people.' And he feels the power of his god and sees the unseen ghost among the people. Then he yelps: 'The god is with us!' And the comedy continues.

"'<'Then, a noble Yoboan replies: 'He is indeed!' He yells: 'His god is with him!' But now, the seriousness of the priest transcends reality.

"'<''Do you see our god?' says the priest.

"'<'The Yoboan says truly: 'No, I don't see your god. Your god is a lie in my eyes.'

"'<''And can you see a lie?' the priest says sarcastically.

"'<''No, my friend, that's why my eyes cannot see him.'

"'<'The beasts accompanying the priest say: 'you will burn in hell.' the priest looks at a sheet of tobacco and from it they extract another carved prophecy.

"'<''Do you understand the words of god now?' The priest says after he repeats the prophecy in an unknown language to the Yoboan and to his own companions; and the chief laughs at their saying. They insist: 'Do you have no ears for the words of truth? Then you will burn in hell!'

"'<'The chief's friends laugh at their ridiculous warning. And again, they ask: 'Do you still deny the existing of our god, our god that created man to his image.'

"'<'And the Yoboan Chief laughs again and then says: 'I do.' Then they aim their powerful weapons at his tribesmen and the messenger of their almighty god declares: 'Then you shall burn in hell.' The foreign warriors take the chief forcefully by the hands and they tie his hands and legs with Taino ropes. They construct a matrix of sticks and light a fire and throw the Yoboan cacique in the demonic fire. As his flesh is melting, the cacique wails in the dry air and his teeth screech as a human, a human being burning in the hell of the strangers.

"'<'Now, the chief's tribesmen are stagnant at the point of deadly weapons, and they are momentaneously speechless. Then, a sudden aaaah! in unison came out of their throats. The priest of the falsely righteous men came upon the witnesses and asks: 'Do you, savages, repent of your major sin?'

"'<'One of the Yoboans, still trembling says: 'Your highness, what sin?'

"'<'The first and most terrible of all of them,' he says. 'The denial of the only true and living God! Answer me truly.'

"'<''I do, my lord. I do believe in your god.' He is pardoned in the name of their god. He murmurs as he untangles himself from the hands of the soldiers:

'These fools think I am going to sentence my own very wise soul.' But then the priest approaches another man, and he asks him the same question. The man is stunned at the images of evil and he can't speak at all.

"'<'So, the priest says to his public: 'The devil has eaten his tongue, throw him into the burning fire.' And the rest of the ex-chief's tribesmen speak of eternal salvation and their likeness to the true god, while the priest's companions chop hands and necks for the sake of their true precious god. My dream ends there.

"'<'My Queen, your husband, my own brother, and his new wife might be crafting the future doomsday of our nations; they say one thing and do the opposite; they talk of peace and send their warriors to eternal war; they claim that lying is a sin, and their own system of beliefs is based on a lie. I wish no harm to my brother, but I come here to Jaragua looking for an alliance to save his life. He and his goddess must return to his town and to his people; for this dream cannot come true; as it is a comedy in my eyes.'

"'<'It is indeed a comedy and a dream, my chief,' the queen ascertains. 'The queen of Yaguana brought a constituent of this mere audience to awe with a dream similar in elements, but dramatic instead of comical. The destruction of our nations is not coincidental, the similar disquieting dream is rather very inspirational, but, my chief, the authors both claim falsely to have sprung a son that is by nature prophetical. What is prophetic about a reality?'

"'<'My child, my child,' Naca says to the queen. 'The time of night asks us to sleep our impatience and desperation away. My dream must have been comical, but its content and its coincidence with the queen's dream, and the witness of people with good eyes and ears, are the elements that bring forth this prophecy. O Queen, I can only tell you that a young cacique once stood in front of a crowd and foretold that a horrible dream, seeming real, would awaken our minds and bring a fight over the belief of a god or a goddess; that strange people in these realms would bring their deities and use them as excuses to extinguish a conquered race. Since then, our ears and eyes, ancient and proud, have been vigilant.'

"'<The queen speaks: 'Oh, powerful man, let not these events in Yoboa conquer your mind. Your brother is not a stranger to these lands, nor is Teteyoa. The great Yagua will never destroy his own blood. Let not your army shed unnecessary blood, a quiet war can be more devastating than the pompous and showy war of men. A contrivance has been engendered by women to overthrow the evil force enthroned invisibly in Yoboa. Though you have a right to impose laws in Yoboa, the god has chosen this place, your own backyard, as a sanctuary of peace and purity; yet war reigns there. Sleep this night in Yassika and return to your land

without further stir, and I promise you the return of a powerful king to his people.'

"'<Now, the cacique agrees partially. Then he says: '. . . that I cannot do. I have already signaled a visit to the great Yaguana. I must hear different arguments. But your argument, fermented with the desire of women, will be supported with all my honor and all my heart.' There you have my part— conjecture its complement from other lips.> The Jaraguan chieftain ends.

Land and Soul

Death of a Noble Queen

XII

"'The hands of a god prolong the arrival of the Maguanan king to Yaguana. Stormy clouds are blown over the desolate Jaraguan sky; thunders in the dark night keep the cacique in Yassika for a few days. But the king is treated graciously by kind and wise Anaya.

"'Then, the hands of the god of clarity sweep the dark clouds from Yassika and pile them one on top of the other over the small region of Yaguana. The queen, past with averaged years, coughs and sniffles, and she feels a fever uncommon and lacking in the souls of young people. The voice that yearns for warmth calls for the missing Yaguanael.

"'The white smoke from bonfires rises to the clouds and messengers cross the welcoming paths of

208

Jaragua; they carry the news of royal eminent death and a self-inviting call to rush with flowers to Yaguana.

"'Soon, a true prophet is heard, crazy as he might seem, in every cluster of huts and in every yucayeque, saying: <O Queen, your moral sayings and your moral stories, propelled only by Taino lips, will shamefully be forgotten in the years of darkness; o Queen, once fair and jovial, now weary and frail, exponentially decaying and gravely pale, rest in peace.>

"'The Royal cacique of Maguana and Anaya, drawn by the sad news, come to Yaguana as quick as lightning, and meet lesser caciques from all Jaragua in the *caney* of her majestic. Unlike her wish, commoners and nobles are seen weeping. But the grief subdues hearts across the realm, remembering the one that was brilliantly artistic.

"'A human dark feeling descends hard on a soft soul, and its heavy influence dents the thoughts of him that is weak. A commoner in a tilt *bohio* lectures the first son of the cacique and advises him of greatness. He says to him: <Your mother, first, princess of the Taino people, then, the Queen of Jaragua, lies suffering on a bed, waiting for your father to come and say goodbye before she closes her eyes forever. Is he a human? Doesn't bad news travel faster than lightning? Isn't that place called Yoboa the center of gossips? He will not come to

say goodbye and she will die. But you shouldn't look at an opportunity as an evil. You are the cacique's son. Go to the *caney* and receive your mother's mourners. Claim a throne that has been abandoned.>

"'Like a dumb spirit the son of the Great Yagua rushes into the *caney* and in front of Yaguanael's true brother, beloved wife, and loyalists says these words: <My mother suffers, and her spirit waits there on that hard bed of straws for my missing father; has he not heard the thunders in the heavens? Is he not a man born of a goddess? I deny all these lies. Where is that man, born of a goddess, which has not been seen in a year in his realm? Am I to stand and weep as a commoner, or am I to claim a rotten monarchy by force?>

"'And Naca, his uncle, says: <Fool, have you not heard that the man you claim to be missing is among us? Ask the nation about its leader, and you will hear the name of your father echoing even in dirty air. It is not he that I fear, for he is as strong as a rock, he is indeed born of a goddess. I fear you and your descendants. But I also see in you a courageous heart, which I fear, for your mind lacks coordination with it. Some wars are not won in a battlefield, my son. Some wars are not lost in a physical war, my son. Trust in your father, for he will always, like a bird in a wild forest, look for your survival. This you should fear, beasts will mistakenly land in this island, and they will claim to be men of peace, but they will hold mortal weapons

in their hands, and your people will innocently
kneel and won't be able to see their heads rolling
on. Their king, the most terrible of kings, invisible,
unharmed by weapons, will guide them on. My son,
your father is not a god, but the things I say come
from his mouth. He is in Yoboa strengthening an
idea that will inoculate us all; he is not lost; he is
with us. But his enemies are not with us and we will
protect him from danger. Now, you will not inherit
his throne, for he will come back to Yaguana, and
he will know that you can easily be fooled. So I say
to you, mourn your mother, and mourn her well, for
she has been deprived of the touch of our deities
and she will soon only be in our memories. And
another thing, my nephew, I fear that that invisible
king will be the king of kings and an old Taino
prophecy will be fulfilled in the time to come. For
this, I say, you are a fool for not believing in your
own father. Even your mother who lies dying there
in that bed of straw believed in him all her life.>

"'<Oh, you fool, you call yourself my uncle. Isn't
that my mother that will stay still as a rock, as still
as nothing, as still as the words my own father told
me, that one day I would see the worst and yet the
best of a dynamic nation? The worst I see; a mother
dying without honor, for what honor does he give
her when she dies without him? I want my mother
to be honored.>

"'Now Anaya stands angrily in front of the Queen's
sons and daughters, and she talks as if in a
soliloquy: <Time, that faculty of the goddess that

211

has bestowed so much grace upon such excellent an integral soul, cuts off her speech; she cannot even softly say goodbye; that speech that used to wake sleeping souls in men and women and endow them with hope and simplicity is gone; eloquent and poetic speech that enlivened the solemn or joyful time; time that is both generous and cruel to both living and inanimate things; that time that gives our goddess an eternal life; that same time of pleasure and pain has decided to be cruel and painful at the ending moment of the noble Queen. But must we let time, which by its own nature cannot be empty, be full only of grief and pain? Once dead, she should be remembered with her songs and her sayings, with her hopes and her visions; so let us feed time with joy instead of grief, with music instead of unwonted silence, and that is honor. And let us . . . ,> a sudden cry cuts her speech off and its solemn content proclaims the queen's death.

"'Now, the king of Maguana interrupts the acute silence and he continues Anaya's discourse: <. . . And let us take her body in a procession to Yoboa and bury her there. Let fix her memory in the mind of every child and make that memory a goddess— eternal until the end of our time; and that is honor.>

"'The queen's son proclaims: <No, no, I would not call you a fool, now, for proclaiming such an honor; but my mother is dead and I will bury her in Yaguana, and that is real honor.>

Land and Soul

Tragedy of Yoboa

XIII

"'Meanwhile, Yoboa keeps growing and growing; the once quiet cluster of huts becomes now a town with a *batey*. The fiesta is on. Borikén, all Kiskeya, and that island north and west that would produce a man of courage and would embrace the spirit of the Taino people all have visited the pious land. This is what it would be now and this is what it would be then; the people of these islands, regardless of origins, will be combatant and passionate; though we will forget the good time, and someone will always remember our nightmares; we will always be in spirit alike.

"'So, the Taino tambour thuds in every corner of Yoboa because the son of the sun will be born from a rebel. The town is decorated with blue, white, and red colors and they will remain in the heart forever. Now, as if in any Taino town, the fiesta goes on every night; but Yoboa will be the mother of

Yagua's son. So, they build a bonfire twice the
usual size and liquor and talks and mixed human
affairs are discussed and put in action; pleasure is a
precious gift from the heaven. The Jaraguan style
carnival brings joy.

"'Yaguana is mourning and there is a voice in the
wilderness that protects aloud against the fanfare
and the spectacle of politics. The king of Maguana
and the queen of Yassika cannot quiet him down.
So, the son screams in mid-forest, his voice sparks
ardent spurts of sorrow and his anger aims invisible
arrows at the present and missing caciques. The
body and insignificant treasures of the famous and
loved queen are dropped to the ground by the
spoiled folks. Suddenly, the disinherited prince and
his misguided mop of commoners erupt like a
volcano and the lava sweeps the bodies of innocent
people. In mid forest the procession is divided and
the dead queen is seized by one side and then by the
other. So the fight continues until they get to the
point where the evil part of nature takes side and the
procession goes on; behind the procession is the
dead body of the queen— in front the happy file of
people in a predetermined rain. The rain and
thunders and dark clouds separate factions. The son
of Hurricane, if a man can invent such an
appellation under the cloudy heaven, howls through
the forest; thunders roar and lightning strikes
between the already-separated factions. The king of
Maguana marches on from the adverse rain; and a
clear day emerges in the horizon. A celebration with
liquor and music, made from raw wood and stones,

(in the present of the spirit of progression) emanates from the unfortunate situation; and the dead one is forgotten.

"'Somewhere behind in the forest the voice of the disinherited one exclaims: <Oh, Yucahu, how can you be so cruel! I am nothing but a man that stands in the rain, guiding a dead corpse, the woman I used to call my mother! I have clearly inherited the dead. Oh, mother of the universe, let the rain stop and let us dig a hole and bury this stinking corpse.> But fate hears him not, and the rain continues; and the procession ahead goes in double steps to Yoboa.

"'Now, Yucahu, dressed as a commoner, for from the voices of the commoners the nobles feed, disguises himself as the companion of a drunkard, and the inebriated one says to the blowing air: <My friend, my unknown friend, look at the stars and you know not if the night is cold, look at the words of the common people and you know not the shapes they mold, feel your blood and give it thoughts and you will comprehend that I am a bitter man, perhaps, if you have a human heart. Then, look at your actions, and you, your highness will understand the message of my companion. Oh noble one, your nobility is not a seal upon your forehead; it is nothing but an evanescent quality that is even present, from time to time, in a drunk like myself, for from time to time, your highness, the symbols upon that body of yours do not reflect your ignoble actions; and therefore the one disguised as a noble man is nothing but a commoner.> Then, he sings:

216

<The memories of the noble one
Shielded by a few bitter days gone—
Everything will be thrown to oblivion
While I celebrate among the 'moral ones.

<Liquor for the honorable Queen of Yassika,
Cohoba for the cacique of Maguana,
Unremembered memories for Jaragua,
And war and vengeful death for Teteyoa.>

"'The words of the man are not ignored by the messenger of the god, for they are heard by the cacique as a sign of warning. So, the cacique moves as swift as the wind, but as smooth as a snake, and approaches the charming queen, who is surrounded by contrivance herself, and says these words: <Anaya, you study the stars and actions of people, have you not thought of ours recently? Although we thought that the quarrelsome prince would catch up to us, his image has been lost for some days. The healers and the attentive people of your realm surround you now, and the smell of a rotten queen is not forgotten now. Oh, dear queen, our intention might seem peaceful, but our march on to Yoboa, with thousands of warriors, behiques, and lawyers reflects nothing but its true form, a war on a holy land. Don't you forget that religious people are the fiercest of warriors? What do you say my dear ally, if we stop and consider cautions and consequences?>

"'And the Queen: <Indeed, your highness, indeed, we have neglected our pledge. Our hope is lame, our actions human. But let us trust in the son of the queen, for nature might have given him the smell of reason. Let us hope that the earth, the one, daughter of our goddess, devour the flesh of the queen, her own daughter, as her law demands. As for us, let us go on to Yoboa together, as a family, and tell our fears to both my husband and his new wife.>

"'<Oh, my queen,> Naca says. <Don't you be naïve, my noble queen. Don't let a lame hope seem to walk straight before you. Have you not heard the drunk speak? Have you lost your wits? Do you warn me against visual violence? Have you forgotten your original plan? I will go back home with my people. I will not enter Yoboa, my own backyard, my land, armed to the teeth against my brother, whom (my spies now say) has proclaimed himself a foreigner and commoner in my land; he's done so for political clarity. My Queen, I beg you, march on in disguise to Yoboa. Poison with herbs that woman that is nothing but trouble to your people. I will enter Yoboa to support you, but not after I hear the tragic news. So go on, choose a mask, one of sorrow, one of happiness, one of piety; go on and choose a mask that fits you for the world will (from now on) be a carnival of politicians. Let the god be with us.> And he says no more.

"'Meanwhile, the forsaken prince in the forest sees the sky clears, but the dark clouds of vengeance remain in his mind and as they bury his dear mother, tears and sniffles emerge from his bent pains. So he says: <Mother, I inter your body in the

earth because you belong to her now. Let her consume you as quickly as she can, for your flesh, skull, and bones are good nutrients for those that will come. But let me pledge in front of you that can't hear, and in front of you, friends, that she will not be the only one to be fed to the recycler of our nature.>

"'A companion says: <But master, we will be outnumbered. Your uncle is the master of war, a strategist by nature. Anaya is a warrior, the fiercest woman in this realm. We have no chance of winning.>

"'The hurt prince replies: <We will put our mask of friendship and slay everyone with the voice of commanding, and the commoners will kneel before us, and they will know I am the heir of Jaragua and the conqueror of Maguana. You, my dear companions, will be rewarded well.>

"'Now murmurs travel from ear to ear and they pledge false allegiance. But one warrior, still loyal to the prince's father, says to another man: <His mother's death and his uncle betrayal have made him mad. We cannot go along with this suicidal idea. For god's sake, someone has to stop his lost mind; he's flying in a dream; somebody has to wake this mad man because if he isn't stopped, death will come to us all, and we will be honoring his ideas and not his once sharp-witted mother, the one that gave us hope and dream and reason. Let's not allow

this man to impose on us the burden of a personal impossible wish—a battle against a mighty god!>

"'The other warrior says: <Hush! My friend. Hush! Your thoughts came too late. His spirit has invigorated his companions; he will call you a coward; they will call you a coward; this happens very often among peers. Play along, because, perhaps, that is exactly what the others are doing; to ease his pains, to console his soul. His mother, the great queen of Jaragua, should not be forgotten; that should be our motto. This man before us is not a leader but a mad man; he looks to aggrandize his position, for the sake of soothing his own spirit, while the better ones, Anaya and his father, his uncle and his mother's friends, look to make a better nation. Play along, my friend, play along, for Yucahu, the god of reason, even after an unreasonable war, will side with the good people.>

=====================================

"'A remarkable man always finds his way to the top; this gift comes to Yagua straight from divine providence. Yoboa has a new master of ceremony; Yagua, a foreigner from Jaragua. But from time to time the god has surprises even for the wisest man. A prophetess from *Borikén*, the land of the valiant lord, comes to a Yoboan *areito*, and her voice is heard among the pious crowd, asking: <Where are you, lord of this land? I have been sent to you with an oracle. Where are you, valiant cousin of my lord? A dream has come to be and I am come here to . . .>

"'A voice from within the crowd interrupts with a question and a comment: <Are you a prophetess, then? Guess who the man you are seeking is.> Laughs and scorns mingle with the rumbles of the tambours; and then they apologize for they think she was mocking them; but upon seeing that she is truly a stranger from another land, though a mere Taino woman, they embrace her and honor her with a place among the most prominent.

"'<You, my lord,> she says. <You are the one I am looking for.> She kneels to praise Yagua. <I had a dream I must deliver to you for they say that you can interpret dreams truly or make them come to fruition with actions.>

"'<My lady, you are much mistaken, like yourself, I am just a foreigner here. Nonetheless, I can interpret your dream, but only god has the power to make it come true. I am not a god. I do not believe in prophecies in the same way as some people do. With the right elements, donated by my god, people can put an oracle together. So the seer might be the source of evil or of virtue. Shoot me with your oracle, my lady.>

"'The dark clouds disappear from the heaven. Snakes and crickets and humans scrawl and hop near the seer; the tambour thuds in the distance and the güira shrieks. And now the prophetess says these words: <My lord, my dream then should be no prophecy. But take these images and tell me if they have meanings: after a big tempest, the blue sky

took dominion over Kiskeya. A voice in the wilderness announce the coming of the pale ones upon the gentle shore; three huge sharks carry ninety evil creatures on their back; they then become huge canoes that land upon Kiskeya's shores. But then, my lord, the wind clears my dream and in the forest I see the birth of two leopards, friendly and gentle, but proud in spirit, just delivered from their mother's womb. And, my lord, sad is the event I came to see . . .>

"'<Say no more, woman, your prophecy has been repeated in these realms a thousand times. For the sharks I will say nothing. But the leopards are the children my wife carries in her womb. Twins she will have! Let them be twins!> He now shouts to the crowd. <Believe me, they will not be pale and they will not be evil.> Then he looks on the crowd, and there, there he sees the old woman that has been the midwife of all his children. <Woman, you there, oh dear friend, have you not recognized the face of this poor man. Come here, oh woman, come here and hug an old friend. I have always known that my goddess is on my side, for the stars shine and the time is opportune upon this hour. Let Yoboa, with permission of my dear absent brother, rejoice! Viva Kiskeya! Oh my great Haiti, how much luck can your grace shed upon me!>

"'Now the carnival refreshes itself and the music and the dances emerge on all Yoboa. In the caney, protected by her warriors, Teteyoa sighs with relief when she hears that the people rejoice in her name;

but she cannot suppress the cries of birth within her, and as the cries explode, Yoboa rejoices even more. Then, the midwife comes into the shielded *caney*; among her servants, masked Anaya shines with flowers and venomous herb.

"'The slow poisonous herb quenches the pain a woman feels. The cries of a male baby first, and then those of a beautiful girl impose their pleasant presence in the intensive room of the *caney*. Rumor flows out of the *caney*, and murmurs spread the true gossip, the queen has delivered two healthy children— a prophecy completed.

"'A measured devil inside Teteyoa begins to interfere with her thinking and delirium battles her senses, but the leafy bed on the ground supports her for the moment. Outside the *caney*, the crowd, dressed with impatience, chanting patriotic songs, inquires with desire and wishes to see the blessed one with her children. Yagua complements his over-enjoyment with talks and liquors, and the crowd goes on chanting and dancing for hours. Queen Teteyoa gathers her strength and stands up and walks out of the imprisoning room into the crowd; at her right side, Queen Anaya with her boy, and at her left the midwife with her girl. A joyous gasp fades to oblivion and then the crowd stands aghast at the crying of a demon, swayed by bitterness, which rushes from the forest with a lance in his hands and pierces through the belly of the poisoned queen. Cries of amazement and cries of war, cries of pains and cries of unpleasantness, cries of all

kinds and dimensions erupt in all Yoboa. Teteyoa's
loyal warriors jump into the war. Cana's warriors
rush into the chaos. Lances land in skulls, arrows
pierce hearts, stone axes chop off legs and arms,
throats are slit with rough knives, men fight even
the harmless wind to survive . . . at the end of the
night, only the strongest survive.

"'The goddesses Apito and Zuimaco have protected
their children well. Proud Cana and harmless Anaya
stand in the mist of corpses while Yagua, still
blaring out of rage, almost rupturing his nerves,
repeatedly lands and lifts his tight-fisted hands on
the beautiful Teteyoa. The survivors begin to feed
the dead to the earth, but they dare not touch the
dead queen, for his beloved will mourn her forever.
Then whispers blame Yagua for all that have been
lost, and they accuse him of abandonment and of
becoming a god. All past events are revealed to him
while he mourns his love and he gets up and says
these words: <Are you not people of the forest?
When has a strong tree forgotten his roots? Have
you not experimented moving a spirited tree from
his habitat? O you people, a foreigner does not
forget his roots; he expands it; it is after all his
survival, for without his beliefs he falls like a
rootless tree. You have faith and your faith is like a
fart in the wind; ours is the pleasant air that we
breathe, the sight of the slanted mountain, and the
curved waves of the sea, the fear of the action of
beasts; yes, like men and women. Now, go on and
show me a lesson. Unbury the thought of the rotten

woman buried in the forest and cut off the head of the freshly dead one, and make a goddess from her skull and call that zemi by name Guamalú; and she will be remembered for what she is, but not in Yoboa but in Yaguana. She will certainly remind my children not to believe in this god you believe I am becoming: a memory implanted in the head of people: an image with legs, arms, a human head, a golden crown, in a mystic place, and with magical power. Is that the god you fear? You should for he is not a harmless image. O Tainos! Don't ever forget these moments, for they are the strength of our roots. Fear me well.> That same night he takes his goddess and he abandons the holy land of Yoboa. Now, the great chief of Jaragua, a warrior with arms and words, is returned to his people. But in the years to come, to the present day, a pilgrimage with fasting people, led by the great cacique of Jaragua and his warriors come to Yoboa. However, as you might be informed, the festivities in Yoboa are past; your brother won't be seen here for another whole year.' Though end the Cacique's nephew.

Deception and Alliance

XIV

"Cibael, the righteous and prudent, the excellent and cultured, the peaceful and humble, born of a goddess, must now come to term with his humanity. His mind's eyes are blinded and confounded by the touching tales of Jaragua. Now, his heart, hurting, pricked by a spear of hope, bleeds nostalgia, worries, and culpability. His youth, felt by years of graces and unnoticed fortunes, now, gone in the moment of a tale, accompanies him not in the time of peril. Nonetheless, youth in the *areito* dances and drinks, and neglects his duty of accountability. So, the old man sees this moment as part of the revealed prophecy. He grabs his nephew by an arm and says: 'Yoboa! You must lead me to Yoboa!'

226

"'What's in Yoboa?'

"'Faith, passion, and war.'

"'War? Have you not come here in peace?'

"'Yes. But in order for us to see peace we must see the end of a war clearly. I fear the prophecy foretold is true. We must invade Yoboa! And you must help me.'

"But why Yoboa?'

"'Because it still stenches like a foul religion. I need a strong alliance to save the nations of Kiskeya. We must unite and go to war against some evil invaders. Help me, son, I urge you.'

"'I am but a lost child that stands in the mid of confusion. Have you gone mad? My chief, with all due respect, my great chief, an invasion of Yoboa would be the least welcome strategy to convene an alliance. Yagua will not fight outside of Jaragua anymore, except in his beloved Yoboa, by a pact of brotherhood and common interests, for in Yoboa laws are secretly made for an entire culture. By invading Yoboa you would bring these brothers of yours together, but as allies against an invader, you or whoever he would be; for Yoboa is a huge shining pearl, shared by these realms. Invasion! Are you not looking for alliances?'

"'Indeed, my bright nephew. Will they join me by a sense of peace or will they join me for a need of war? Let us dig a few holes to bury the dead, and people will come crawling to bury themselves. We must train ourselves to fill the tenantless tombs with dirt wherever a digger labors, and fear the notion of the future. Oh, my nephew, we must bring fear again to Yoboa, for it has inoculated our souls against the control of strangers. The rod to measure greatness in a cacique reaches only to his shoulder and the head of a great cacique is measured by the hope he gives to his people, the fear he instills in the innocents, and the good actions that end in excellence, and no more. Isn't this a world of reverse abstractions: war to secure peace? Fear is like a whip in the hand of the good master; hope is the food that quenches fear and gives obedience, and good actions are the nobilities of the soul. War brings brothers together. Show me Yoboa!'

"'Oh, my dear uncle, do not make me a traitor. Try the peaceful way and I promise you alliances. Your brothers love you.'

"'But how long will this peaceful way take to lead me where I am going? I fear time is a scourge; there must be a faster way. I can pave a smooth path to conviction. Ah! Yucahu, god of inventions, show me the path I seek. My nephew, can you make my troops and my presence be a secret here? I also need to know of your allegiance. I promise you, you will be remembered as a hero, for it is not I that seek your trust and allegiance, but the sacred and intrepid Kiskeya.'

"'I will. Let us sleep tonight and let your fresh reflection reconsider your contrivance. I will follow your commands.'

"The festivities come to a close and soon sleep invades heavily on all the subjects of the region. And the night shrinks quickly and Bajacu whistles with the entrance of the sun and the tweeting of the little birds. All Maguan warriors and their leader change their plumage in their heads, and they change the smears in their faces, and then they undo their makeover to look again like Maguans. Now, they switch coloring and clothing and they resemble Maguanans as they are led to Yoboa. In their way, Cibael instructs his nephew and his nephew the captains and the captains the performers.

"As they encounter wandering Maguanan warriors, the Maguans are silent and the Nephew screams in greeting: 'Hey there, let Yucahu be with you! Maguana is made stronger for your service. I thank you. We come in peace and love to strengthen the spirit of Yoboa. Adieu.' And once they pass the warriors, he says: 'Cao, Ambix, Caeli, and Cix, come here quickly. You are to sprint as quickly as the waterless clouds in a windy day, and invade Jaragua's closest towns. Cao and Ambix, take the goddess of Rumor and stimulate her with words of doomsday; make her instills fear in the weakest and avoid contact with all things that seem noble. Caeli

and Cix, split as far as you can, as quick as you
may, and when rumor passes your way, for she is
thrice a thousand times quicker than a human's
pace, hurry and burn a few huts here and there.
Don't hesitate and fly back as quickly as the speedy
wind; we will all change appearance and pretend to
have crippled the fierce and powerful Yoboa.'

"Cao and Ambix meet talkative people in Jaragua,
they begin to tell a thousand lies; the first goes like
this: '. . . and a huge fire descended from the sky
and burned half the region of Macorix, and gods
came upon the shore from the sea and enslaved all
the people there.' And to a fanatical group of people
they say: '. . . and they ride on a quick, strong, and
agile ungentle beast as fast as lightning.' And yet to
another group they say: '. . . they have now spread
through the island and captured Holy Yoboa.'

"Jaragua starts to burn and she wakes up and jumps
quickly to her feet as Rumor gets to Yaguana. 'My
chief, my great chief,' a warrior, taken prisoner by
Rumor, panting and running toward the caney, says:
'Kiskeya has been invaded. Yoboa the free and
eloquent has been muted and enslaved. Black
smokes are burning in Higüey and Magua. Marien
seems to know nothing of the tragedy and I have
ordered the signals to avert its people of the threat.'
He pants some more.

"Now, the cautious king arises calmly from his
leafy couch. 'What of Jaragua?' he inquires.

"The warrior says: 'She burns, my chief. Chaos is everywhere.'

"'Is Yaguana burning, too?'

"'They say she is, my great chief.'

"'They say she is! What do you say?'

"'I say nothing, my chief. I have seen people running and calling the goddess of Mercy, Zuimaco, and the chief of Jaragua; that's all I have seen.'

"'Are the twin bonfires of Yoboa burning?'

"'Yes, my chief. The threat is real.'

"The chief stands up and runs outside to see the smoke of a secret pact fuming in the air, forming the clouds of war and alliances. But now, he feels abandoned by his goddess; his face reflects his age; he knows that the goddess's magic works better in the presence of the new. Nonetheless, this might be his last battle. Soon enough, Yaguana's sirens, palms bumping on every mouth and exhaling and inhaling tireless lungs blowing and shrinking fill the realm of Jaragua. Every able body becomes a warrior; canoe paddlers run to the sea to protect the shores and the forest is invaded by courageous people.

"The news is belated in the Coral of the Indians, Maguana's chief is unaware of the false invasions.

But Rumor, that quick and sneaky creature, who is unable by her nature to sit and rest, comes urgently to Cana's door. The chief quickly runs out of his caney; age has now become a clutch, a burden. But his goddess gives him the strength to realize that nothing lasts forever; Kiskeya, in his heart, must yet survive a thousand and a thousand years before its unification. So, the sirens standardized in Yoboa ring through the realm. Bonfire signals are sent to the brave Higüey and to Magua, and Magua responds with friendly smokes, aiming to Marien, Maguana, Jaragua and Higüey. Yoboa must be regained!

"Propaganda and deceit are two powerful weapons. The daylight sees thousands of disguised warriors running up and down the roads. The belief that the town has been captured, a belief spread by rumor and stupid mouths, cower the warriors in duty; the mothers see evils everywhere there is tranquility, and the old resent their youth, for they cannot fight, and they themselves, seeing nothing, believing something evil, think they are blind. So Yoboa is captured by the great Cibael, disguised as a stranger. But when the goddess throws her black blanket called night in the quiet, peaceful, and pious town, Rumor, as fast as the speed of light, tells that the cowards are all retrieving to Macorix, their base, because all Kiskeya is conglomerating at once in the Great Yoboa. (Oh, Higher Macorix, have you not given the Taino the wrong impression, Kiskeya would have been a stronger pedestal!)

"Now this huge black cloud captures almost all the hearts of Yoboa; it is like an evil empire, marching and crushing all the poor souls with empty promises. The true invaders have all by now changed their masks and become Maguans and Maguanans. Rumor is sent once again to every corner of Yoboa and quickly it travels to meet the angry warriors of innocence. Rumor takes her invisible trumpet and words proclaim the great cacique of Magua a Hero. For the first time, Kiskeya owes him a favor. Warriors flow in from Magua, from Marien, from Higüey, and from Jaragua; and for the last time, they will all march together as brothers to Macorix, to save a nation.

Oh, Macorix, I don't think I ought to tell of this foreseen Tragedy there." The Queen pauses her story and I wake up from my first dream, wanting more.

END OF THE FIRST DREAM

Names, People, and Foreign Words

Aguacar: The goddess of Magua
Amayauna: a harsh cave in Kiskeya, birthplace of non-Taino Kiskeyans
Amazon: From the Amazon forest in South America
Ambioryx, trusted man of the princess Teteyoa
Anacaona: Taino poetess, narrator of the tales
Anaya: Queen of Yassika, wife of Naca
Apito: Goddess of Maguana
Areito: Nightly ceremony celebrated by the Taino
Arixis: Favored son of Cibael
Atabeira: Goddess of Higüey
Atabey: the essence of the universe, the goddess of the universe
Bajacu : The goddess of daylight, of the morning
Batey: the ceremonial center of the small town
Batú: Ballgame, main sport of the Tainos
Beata: A Taino island close to Kiskeya
Behique: The healer, doctor, priest of the Tainos
Betai: A fictitious husband of Teteyoa; a rebel
Bohechio: The Cacique of Jaragua during the Spanish conquest
Bohio: a hut, a shack
Boinayel: a god
Borikén: The island of Puerto Rico
Cacarocayoa: Mother of Cayacoa's lineage, cacique of Higüey

234

Cacibajagua: A cave in the mountain of Cauta, birthplace of the Tainos
Cacibajaguan: related to Cacibajagua; from Cacibajaguan
Caney: The large rectangular hut of the cacique
Cao, Ambix, Caeli, and Cix: Maguanans helping Cibael
Caobana: The Taino name of the island of Cuba
Cariban: pertaining to the Caribs tribe
Caribbean Sea: An Atlantic Ocean sea, bounded by North, central and South Americas
Caribs : Tribes from the Lesser Antilles
Cassava: Yucca bread
Cauta: The fictitious mountain in Kiskeya, origin of the Tainos
Cibael: Royal Cacique of Magua in these tales
Cibao: Another name for Magua
Cibaons: pertaining to the people or region of Cibao
Ciguayan: adj. pertaining to the people of Macorix
Ciguayos: the native people of Macorix
cinzontle: a North American bird
Coaybay: the land of the dead
Cohoba: A drug inhale with a pipe, similar to cocaine
conucos: a small cultivated field
Coral of the Indians: The capital of Maguana
Dujó: the decorated seat of the nitainos
Guabance: The goddess of flood, companion of Hurricane
Guacanael: an ancient cacique

Guacanarix: The cacique of Marien during the Spanish conquest

Guacar: the goddess of Magua

Guamalú: a goddess of memories and histories, invented by Yagua

Guanahani: the name the natives gave to the island that Christopher Columbus called San Salvador

guanin: a lucky Taino bracelet

Guárico: place in Marien, capital of Marien

Guarionex: The cacique of Magua during the Spanish conquest

Guatauba: a messenger of the god

Güiras: a Taino musical instrument

Higüey: one of the five chiefdoms of Kiskeya

Holy Hill: The capital of Magua

Hurricane: The evil god of storm and destruction

Itahura: a Maguan sent in an expedition to Macorix

Jaragua: one of the five chiefdoms of Kiskeya

Kiskeya: Taino name of the island of Hispaniola

La Vega: Region of Cibao

La Vega's Royal Valley: the valley of La Vega, in Cibao

Lineri: A Maguan sent in an expedition to Macorix

Macocael: a fictitious ancient cacique

Macorixians: from the region of Macorix

Macorix: a region in Kiskeya, land of the Ciguayans

Macuto: a small bag worn in the field

Magua: one of the five chiefdoms of Kiskeya

Maguan: related or pertaining to Magua

Maguana: one of the five chiefdoms of Kiskeya

Maguanan: related or pertaining to Maguana
Maketaori: the overseer of Coaybay
Maorocoti: another name for Yucahu; a god
Marieanel: the fictitious cacique of Marien in these tales
Marien: one of the five chiefdoms of Kiskeya
Mother *Iermao* : the goddess of Marien
Naca: short for Nacanarocoel
Nacanarocoel: the cacique of Maguana
Nitainos: the noble class in Taino society
Kiskeya: island of Hispaniola
Quisqueyan: related or pertaining to Kiskeya; same as Kiskeyan
Riyamuy: a Maguan sent to Macorix
Saona: an island close o Kiskeya
Siboney: a tribe in Kiskeya and Cuba
Soursop: a fruit
Taino: People who inhabited several islands in the Caribbean Sea
Teteyoa: A Siboneyan princess; then a Taino queen
Yagua: short for Yaguanael
Yaguana: capital of Jaragua
Yaguanael: the royal cacique of Jaragua
Yananini: a man invented in a tale by Teteyoa
Yaquimo: a region in Jaragua
Yassika: Anaya's village,
Yoboa: the biggest ceremonial center in Kiskeya
Yoboan: pertaining to Yoboa
Yucahu: the main god of the Taino people
Yuna: A river in Macorix
Zemi: word equivalent to god
Zui: a region in Jaragua
Zuimaco: the goddess of Jaragua

Land and Soul